The Crystal Ball

A Micki Michaels Mystery

Joyce Mason

THE CRYSTAL BALL
A Micki Michaels Mystery

© 2013 by Joyce Mason
All Rights Reserved
New Inkarnation Media™
First Edition, November 2013
ISBN: 978-0-615-89461-4

newinkarnation.com

Cover design by Karen Phillips Covers
phillipscovers.com

Cover background art © phokrates - Fotolia.com

Mask © piai - Fotolia.com

Interior design by Pretty Road Press
PrettyRoadRress.com

For my fathers

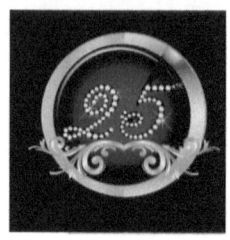

The Immortalists on Planet Earth Association
requests the honor of your presence
at our costume gala

The Crystal Ball
on December 31st
8:00 PM until dawn

The Moonlight Ballroom
144 Pacific Shore Drive
San Francisco, California

Celebrate the New Year and the
Silver Anniversary of IOPEA's
25 years of accomplishments.

Theme with prize for the best costume,
"Come as you will be in the future."

Please RSVP to IOPEA
by December 15th

"Love is the reason for longevity."

~ The Immortalist's Handbook

Chapter 1

My Tibetan chime alarm clock pulsed soothing tones throughout my Victorian bedroom. Soft vibes resonated in all directions, slowly increasing in volume, as if someone had thrown a pebble into a sweet sound pool. Creatures were stirring—dust mites, humans–cat. Then my clock started talking.

"Good morning, Micki. This is Cosma, your multi-dimensional music, sleep, and information center. This is your 7:30 AM wake-up call. Coming up in two minutes is your musical selection, 'Let's Have a Party' by Elvis Presley. The time at the tone is 7:30 AM and 55 seconds, Pacific Standard Time. Today is December 31st. Happy New Year's Eve!"

A louder, single chime sounded as Cosma continued. Her electronic voice was sexy and soothing—almost too mellow for a wake-up call, especially since I'm a night owl. I think mornings are for the birds—any other kind.

"It's time for Planet Watch. The planetary positions at this moment are:

Sun: 9 degrees Capricorn, 32 minutes.

Moon: 23 degrees Aries, 15 minutes ..."

One of my wacky inventor friends created Cosma for me as a birthday gift, a prototype clock of the future, when everyone will know, understand, and care about astrology. Astrologer is my past profession, sometimes my current one. Once an astrologer, always an astrologer like "once a Catholic." I was both to the core, even when I practiced neither.

When Cosma got to "Saturn: 9 degrees Cancer, 47 minutes Retrograde," exactly opposite the Sun, my eyes popped. I was awake now. This unsettling astrological aspect triggered the memory of my ugly dream. I saw a man with a bullet right between his eyes. He was on a stage of some sort. People around him were dressed funny. I suspected they were wearing era costumes, but I couldn't place the period.

At its absolute worst, Saturn can bring death. But isn't Death just Father Time? A guy whose passing we applaud with noisemakers every New Year's Eve, then celebrate the Baby New Year at midnight with kisses and confetti? Maybe my subconscious was just beating Cosma to the punch, telling me, *Hey, Micki. It's New Year's Eve. Wake up and smell the coffee! Organic French Roast. It'll hit you right between the eyes!*

Maybe it was just a bad pizza dream. One of my favorite dreamwork authors says they're common—and meaningless. A bad trip on acid indigestion. With might-mean-nothing as an option, I tucked the dream in the back of my mind to ponder later.

When I first got Cosma in the mid-1990s, she was way ahead of her time. It didn't take long for her to worm her way into my heart, like a family pet. Even better, a pet with no food or vet bills—and no fleas. I hate fleas.

But I love children. Unfortunately, I don't have any—not from lack of wanting them. It just never worked out that way. My name is Michele Nichole Michaels. Micki's my nickname.

Now for my most unusual characteristic. Years ago, my landlady was giving me the lowdown on the elderly woman who lived upstairs. She said, "The years have not been kind to her." You could say just the opposite about me. I'm 50, but I look 30. The reason's easy. I'm an immortalist.

Before you roll your eyes and lump me in with all the other nut cases you have ever known, let me explain. We're called the Immortalists on Planet Earth Association or IOPEA, pronounced *eye-OH-pea-uh*. The proximity in sound to eye-opener is intentional. The headquarters of our organization is in San Francisco—where you see it all and hear it all—Capital of the Left Coast. Some call it Babylon by the Bay. Others say Sodom and Gomorrah. I like to think of it simply as the most original and beautiful place on earth. I'm IOPEA's president.

The overcast winter morning peered through my beveled glass window and the muffled sounds of the City sang backup to Cosma's chimes. At least the City wasn't Playing Misty for Me, as she often did on a winter's morn. I wanted it dry and pleasant for people traveling to and from the Crystal Ball. I felt a chill—but before I could shiver, the phone rang. I dove toward the nightstand to get it on the first ring, so I wouldn't wake up Curt, the man who sleeps next to me. No words came through the earpiece, just breathing—actually, *heavy* breathing. Unsettling. After three hellos, I finally hung up—hard. Damn pranksters. You'd think someone with nothing better to do than to annoy other people wouldn't get up so early to do it. This time, for whatever reason, it sent a chill up my spine that had nothing to do with the weather. It wasn't the first time I'd gotten these crank calls, but I couldn't be sure it was the same crackpot—or pots.

I demanded a change of mood, ordering Cosma, "Tell me something great today." As if on cue, my little astro-clock continued:

"Today's transits for Michele Nichole Michaels are as follows."

When she got to Saturn conjunct Ascendant Retrograde, I sat bolt upright in bed, yelled, "No. No!" then crossed my index fingers, holding my arms out, as if warding off a vampire. Saturn wasn't just in a not-so-hot position for people in general; it was in a particularly scary position for me. Pass the garlic.

"I said say something *nice.*"

My outburst startled Curt awake, the lump under the covers beside me.

He cursed. I'm not sure if it was at Cosma or me.

Curt Stern has been a knot in my stomach since I was 17 years old. Let's start with his most unusual characteristic. My beloved boyfriend retired from the FBI almost a year ago, about the same time he came bopping back into my life out of nowhere, just like nothing had ever happened—again. He was an expert at it, having done it countless times before, when we were kids. Curt did more disappearing and reappearing than Houdini, usually when I'd finally given up on him.

When he broke my heart to smithereens for the last-straw time in our early twenties, I thought I'd never see or hear from him again. For three decades, I didn't. Then in my unresolved grief, I finally tracked him down. I kept having unremitting dreams about him. I found Curt on the same day he started looking for me. I figured it just proved we were still connected at the heart in some magical way. Curt thought it was eerie. I talked about Carl Jung's concept of synchronicity—meaningful coincidence. Curt said there were "loose ends."

What an understatement.

Once he retired and was no longer wed to being near the nation's capital, Curt decided to rent out his condo, move to San Francisco, and move in with me. This arrangement is open-ended, until we figure out if it's what we want. Geographic proximity seemed like the only answer to exploring our relationship. Bi-coastal romances are nothing but a string of honeymoons with hardly any reality checks. It helps that he loves San Francisco.

The phone rang again. I didn't hurry to grab it this time, figuring it was the crackpot, not necessarily more lovely or talkative the second time around.

I was off on a cloud, musing about Curt and me. I know opposites attract, but we are ridiculous. I'm liberal; he's conservative. I'm spiritual—metaphysical with a lot of cutting-edge beliefs. He only believes what he can "see, hear, taste, touch, or … *ravage*." He normally pauses after cleaning up the last word in his favorite catchphrase, then raises his eyebrows and leers at me. Curt's doing his best to show me he's trying to swear off swearing. It's not as if I have virgin ears. Cursing is really a puny sin in my humble opinion. I grew up in a family who expressed themselves verbally, no holds or cuss words barred. However, when the F-word starts flying like mortar fire and is used as often as *the*, it sounds angry and abrasive. It quickly morphs into chronic negativity. I'm sensitive. I have to monitor the energy in my personal space. Curt claims it's habit, how guys talked all the time on his old job. He has certainly convinced me what the F stands for in FBI.

Our differences aside, I know there's something more than great sex that pulls Curt and me together like metal to a magnet. When I figure out what it is, I'll let you know.

I reached over to answer the phone on the cordless next to Cosma, but Curt jumped up with a start and grabbed my arm.

"Don't touch it."

"Why not?"

"Because it might be the creeps that are trying to scare you."

"I hate this, Curt," I said, referring to whoever was harassing key members of IOPEA and sending them bizarre phone messages in coded phrases that reminded me of ransom notes by kidnappers.

I figured crackpots went with the turf on my job. Some people figured IOPEAns were messing with things they shouldn't, playing God, trying to fool Mother Nature. Still, I didn't get why we irked them. We're just people who want to live a long and productive life. I wasn't about to let such vague threats get to me.

But this Mr. Foy, as he called himself, had been the boldest. He was the only one who identified himself by name—and only to me. Foy kept implying that if I didn't cooperate in giving him the secret of immortality, he would harm someone I cared about. He was never specific, so I blew him off.

But I never blow off Curt when he uses his enforcer voice. I jump. I know he has lived in realms where I have absolutely no experience; he has lived through unspeakable dangers. During the final years of his career, Curt worked counterintelligence, a top FBI priority in our post-9/11 nation. He, too, has nightmares.

I let the phone ring through to the recorder, so we could both hear the message. I was glad I had resisted the convenience of voice mail in favor of being able to screen calls live. A sinister, high-pitched voice followed the beep. The beep felt rude after Cosma's sweet nothings masquerading as wake-up tones.

The caller's Irish brogue was so thick and stereotyped; it had to be fake. "Top o' the mornin', Ms. Michaels. This is Mr. Foy, and I know you are there. I thought you'd like to know your niece was on her way to your house, but she didn't quite make it. She didn't make it at all, at all."

I knew which niece he meant, the one who often popped in unannounced to see me on mornings she didn't have school. I tried to reach the phone to talk to this Foy, horror pounding in my ears, but Curt grabbed my wrist hard. He sneered, tightening his anger between his teeth.

"That fuckin' creep." So much for language.

Foy continued, "Know that I am serious, Ms. Michaels. I will call you back in one hour. You must negotiate with me or the little girl and your Crystal Ball will be in grave danger."

The only word I heard was *grave*.

I wrenched Curt's hand off my wrist and grabbed the receiver. "There is no secret," I told Foy. "It's all out in the open in the *Immortalist's Handbook*. Increased youthfulness and longevity don't come from a single lotion, potion or pill. They involve an attitude, a belief system — mind training with a few simple rules for preserving the body thrown in. I have nothing to give you."

"Whisht! Such lies out of your gob. You must think I'm really naïve, missy."

I rankled. I didn't understand all of his Irish expressions, but missy is a diminutive term. I objected. How disrespectful! OK, maybe I'm a little sensitive about my height, hardly 5'3" in my stocking feet. I thought my big personality made up for it.

Foy was working himself into a froth. "No one can shave 20 years off their appearance, as a matter of course, like you IOPEA people do. The last one of you to die was 101. You can't convince me you're not enhancing yourselves and hiding something. You must think me a fool."

Foy was remarkably well read on IOPEA. I thought it best not to say what I thought of him.

"I can't tell you what there isn't to tell!" I knew I was wasting my breath, but I had to try to convince him.

"You'd better pick up your pencil, missy, and write down this fax number. You have one hour from right now to send me the formula or the ingredients of your product or products—or, I repeat, your big affair and your little niece are in danger. That's 8:40 AM. Get on it. And no guards. You call the police or have this call or the fax number traced? You'll find out how much Irish I have."

He slammed down the receiver. My hands shook when I wrote down the number. I had repeated it to him twice, so scared, I could barely see straight.

My stomach dove to my feet, and my heart leapt to my throat, where it was hanging on my tonsils. He had us staked out, and it sounded like he had snatched Tansy. She's only 13, my late brother's granddaughter—the only child of his only daughter, April. This was no longer an innocuous game.

Curt was spewing profanity about how the SOB knew how to get me, how to go straight for my maternal instincts. I'm normally the poster girl for Peace on Earth, but threaten someone I love, and my reactions are knee-jerk and hostile.

"I'm telling you right now; don't even think about handling this guy alone. I remember the dog, Michele."

OK, so once I threw myself bodily across a Doberman Pinscher, which had wandered into my tiny back garden, cornered my cat Methuselah, and was about to go for Thusie's jugular.

"How you got out of that mess without a scratch is a mystery to me. I don't know if you hexed him with one of your woo-woo spells or channeled Dr. Doolittle. But you won't expose yourself to that kind of danger as long as I'm here."

"Who died and left you Lord and Master?"

My outburst blew open the valve to my tear ducts, and I sobbed loudly for several minutes solid, while Curt went back and forth between hugging me and pacing the floor, trying to figure out what to do next. I felt so alone, because Curt's way would be to use guns and force, against everything IOPEA and I stand for. I had to find another way.

I soon realized I had no time for hysteria. How would I get her back? What was I going to tell April?

Shaking, I grabbed my cell phone out of my purse, where I had her on speed dial.

"Micki? You sound funny."

"April, I have something difficult to tell you." I gulped. I could hardly breathe. My mouth was a desert.

"I got this frightening call about Tansy. I know this sounds goofy, but this evil man has been harassing me and other members of IOPEA. He just called and implied he grabbed Tansy."

"You're right, it does sound goofy. She's standing right here." I was so relieved; I nearly wet my pants.

Chapter 2

"hank God! Omigod! Omigod, I've gotta breathe."

After a few rounds of deep breaths, the kind I'd learned in yoga, I continued.

April waited for me regain my composure. She was used to this behavior.

"April, the point is, if she's not in danger now, she could be any minute. Please put her on. We'll talk after I tell her." April balked.

"Forget it. I'm not waiting even a minute to hear the details of what this is all about. I'll put you on speakerphone, so you can tell us both at once."

I could hear April call her over. Tansy, still clueless, sounded all cheery.

"Hi, Aunt Micki!"

I figured Foy's real purpose this morning was to let me know he was watching Tansy, that he *could* grab her at any time, even though he hadn't—yet. Still, I had to confirm it.

"So, what did you do this morning?"

"Well, I was actually on my way to your house. I was almost there when I realized I forgot this thing I wanted to show you, this cool picture of grandpa I found in an old suitcase. I came back for it."

The image of my brother tugged at my heartstrings. It was only five years ago that Gregg died of AIDS. He was my only sibling, a year younger.

"I'd love to see that picture, Tansy, but not today. Too much happening, getting ready for the Crystal Ball and all."

"I can't wait!"

"Well, you just may have to. There's a man threatening me and some other people in IOPEA. I'm not sure it's a good idea for you to be at the party. In fact, I don't want you to leave the house without talking to me first, at least till Curt and I get a handle on what's going on with this guy."

"But Aunt Micki! My costume's great, and Brady and I have been looking forward to this forever."

I hadn't even met Brady yet; her boyfriend was so new.

"I know, Tansy, but safety first. I'll try to work things out so you can go, but I can't promise anything. Now go off and do something else while I talk to your mom alone."

I thought she was going to bawl. I could almost hear her pouting. I felt like a heel.

April pressed off the speaker button, and we talked long enough for her to promise me that she wouldn't let Tansy out of her sight without consulting me. She was a single mom, and I worried about her. I told her Curt and I would see if we could get someone to stay with them, at least until we had a better feeling for what was going on and how careful we needed to be. Maybe we could rig up a bodyguard of sorts—one of Curt's cronies from his makeshift fraternity of cops and former spies.

I hung up feeling drained. New Year's Eve had barely started, and now I had to worry: How would I protect Tansy and everyone at the Crystal Ball from some cuckoo?

Meanwhile, Foy's evil clock was ticking.

The thought made me appreciate Cosma more than ever. I pressed her audio button, just to hear her soothing voice. "The time at the tone is 7:49 AM and 45 seconds."

The time pressure triggered a memory, when I used to call Time to set my clock or watch. The alpha for the number on the phone keypad was POPCORN. Now Foy was going to call time in 50 minutes. My brain needed to start exploding ideas fast, like the kernels in a microwave bag of popcorn. It was time to turn up the heat.

Chapter 3

I started pacing. No time to lose to figure out what to do next.

"Lies are too hard to keep up. It takes too much energy," I said to Curt.

"Huh?"

"I don't have any time. The bastard's only giving me an hour, so I'm thinking out loud. Thinking, then repeating to you everything I thought, takes too long. Please listen and you're welcome to talk when you've got something to add. IOPEA is my responsibility, and I have to come up with a solution to either stall Foy or make him go away permanently.

"That I could help you with," he said.

"No guns, no violence."

"No fun."

"I'm serious, Curt. No lies."

"Liar, liar, pants on fire, hanging over the telephone wire!" Curt and his inner child chanted.

I rolled my eyes.

"I'm sure I know what kind of pants are hanging over the telephone wire of your depraved little mind."

"Thongs, of course ... or G-strings, if you want to dance for me first," he added with a grin so devilish, I knew why these imaginary undies were on fire.

"Back on point, Perv, I won't say anything that isn't true. The option to make up a secret concoction just doesn't work for me. Number One, it's not in my nature to lie. Number Two, it takes way too much effort. Lies get so convoluted. I'd never keep my stories straight."

"You'd make a shitty spy," Curt pronounced.

"This is not a job interview."

I ran my fingers through my shoulder-length auburn hair. Nervous habit. Curt calls it raking my curls. The few times I'd caught a glimpse of myself in a mirror while doing this, I was horrified. With my hair pulled back, my Moon-shaped face looked even rounder. I didn't think that was possible. Without using a few optical illusions, my mug was the same shape as Charlie Brown's head, and I'm not cartooning you.

"OK, here's what I think I should do. I'll fax Foy a formal letter with the link to all the info on IOPEA's web site, promising on my mother's life or my father's grave that this is the whole truth and nothing but. I'll also call Hans Jenner. He's a biochemist. Works for a big biotech firm in Emeryville. He's always dabbling with vitamins and other supplements, trying to mix the master youth tonic, even though it'd probably only be a new blend of stuff we already know about that's available in various forms elsewhere."

"So, what's your thinking here ... what would that do?"

"Stall for time. My intuition tells me Foy is not a scientist, and he'd have to run it by someone else before he'd know what we sent him. Hans can make it full of formulas and complexities, something only another biochemist would understand."

"You're thinking he can make it complicated enough that the guy or his people can't figure it out till tomorrow? Stall through the Ball, so to speak?"

"Depends on who Foy has access to. If he tells me fairly fast that he thinks what I sent him is a bunch of BS, then we know he has brains behind him, scientific ones."

"And what does that do for you?"

"Brings me back to Square One, I guess ... and then I can only hope one of us has a more brilliant idea. I'm praying the guy is more mouth than brains."

"Well, for my part, I think you're overreacting to this guy, Micki. So far, he's been all talk and no action. What has he really done except to let you know he's watching you and your family? Or maybe the people in your office? Worst case, if he continues threatening you, we can always get the police involved, ask for a restraining order and nail him for stalking."

"That'd take too long. That's a long-term plan. We need something now. He's threatening Tansy now and the Crystal Ball is tonight. I'm just not willing to risk either. They're both too important to me, Tansy first and foremost."

"Michele, he's jerking you around, playing on your maternal instincts. He's a creep. Unless this escalates, I think you should just shine him on, forget about him, make passionate love to me, and then get ready to be the Belle of the Ball. I mean, this is fun. I admit it. It gives me a rise I sometimes miss, but only because the stakes aren't as high as you think.

"But what if they are? Curt, I just don't have a good feeling about this."

That's the same thing I told Hans when I called. Instead of giving me "a look," which would have been hard to do over the phone, anyway, he said, "Everyone at IOPEA knows that when you have one of those feelings, it's as good as Moses coming down from the Mount with a new stone tablet."

"Come on, Hans. My intuitions aren't so accurate that you could write them in stone. Stones have no eraser. Sometimes I'm in the ballpark but in the wrong seat. That's how intuition works. There's a lot of interpretation left up to the person with the inklings."

"You're too modest, Micki. I'd say you're downright psychic, and combined with your gift for metaphors and symbols; you're usually on the money."

"Thanks, Hans. But can you actually do what I'm asking? Give him some complex chain of biochemical gobbledygook?"

"I'm sure I can have even a biochemical whiz kid scratching his head for at least an hour or two. Don't know about a whole day and night. But I'll do my best. I can make the handwriting terrible and the formulae scratchy. That can only help."

While Hans started putting together his crude artwork, I went to my computer and composed my missive to Foy. I was so hyped; I never realized I hadn't had a single cup of coffee.

The Immortalists on Planet Earth Association
22 Fanwell Street
San Francisco, CA 94129
www.right2longlifers.org

31-Dec
8:05 AM

Dear Mr. Foy,

Because you have given me only an hour to provide you with this infor-mation, and I live across the Bay from IOPEA's biochemist, Mr. Hans Jen-ner: he will fax his formula to you directly. However, I must reiterate for the record the high points of our earlier conversation. This supplement is not a standalone "fix" that is responsible for the increased lifespan enjoyed by members of IOPEA. The combination of factors that we believe lead to our increased longevity can be found in The Immortalist's Handbook, *which you can download directly from our web site: www.right2longlifers.org. Fol-lowing this letter/cover page are the highlights of a speech I am giving at tonight's 25th anniversary celebration of IOPEA. My talk will reiterate the key principles in the* Handbook *and cite efforts IOPEA has made to further longevity studies in the field of holistic health. I'll also report on our efforts in ecology, since it wouldn't be much fun to live long on a dying planet.*

You will be ahead of everyone at the party, having an advance written summary of my speech, and I hope it will satisfy any reason you might have to consider crashing an invitation-only event, pardon my bluntness.

Finally, Mr. Foy, let's focus on what we have in common. We both care about longevity. However, the concept of a "secret" just doesn't fit into IOPEA's belief system. The option of a long, healthy, productive life should be accessible to all human beings equally. That's why we publish every significant step to achieve it. I am open to any reasonable test to prove to you that this is the truth of the matter—and what we are about. Meanwhile, I hope you begin to work with these tools: attitude, vitamins, diet, exercise and sharing your talents with others.

Wishing you well on your quest,

Michele Nicole Michaels
President

PS — As to how great we look, we are not beyond a few cosmetic nips and tucks here and there, but I doubt you'll ever see one of our members on Extreme Makeover.

Chapter 4

I came out of my home office and headed for the kitchen, where Curt was biting the end of a pencil, doing the crossword puzzle in the *Chronicle*. I could tell he was worried about Foy.

"Well, I did it. I talked to Hans, and I faxed the letter to Foy."

"Uh huh," he said. "What's an eight letter word for a sharp, bitter manner?"

"Acrimony."

Curt gave me his full-face-change, a familiar set of expressions I'd come to interpret over time, starting with a flush of embarrassment, as if I'd just caught him with his pants down. This was always followed immediately by a scowl of irritation, inching slowly into a half-grin of humility. Then he'd top it off with a remark acknowledging my help—or point.

"Always bitter always to ask the word whiz."

Puns and fencing with words were two of my favorite parts of our relationship. Witty repartee was right next to sex.

I got a kick out of watching Curt run his emotional gamut. Humility wasn't his long suit, but he knew I wasn't willing to hide my brains under a bushel just to flatter his ego—and that I shouldn't. This was the kind of chink in his armor that made me hold out hope for him—hope that we could evolve out of the silly set roles from our foolish youth and into a true partnership of equals.

"Speaking of bitter," I said, "how 'bout showing some concern about what I'm going through?"

He sighed. "Sorry, babe, but like I said before, I just can't get too hot and bothered about this guy at this point."

Since the nearest human was irritating me for his lack of empathy, I decided to dump man for machine and buzz for Hazel, my little robo-maid.

This would be a good time to explain that my life is a bundle of contradictions. It's not just the yin and yang of Micki and Curt.

For example, I live in a two-story Victorian built in 1900 in a beautiful neighborhood called Pacific Heights. Only since it's located almost at the bottom of the hilly Heights on the south side, my brother always called it Pacific Depths. I bought into Lower Pacific Heights years ago, before San Francisco real estate went half way to the stars.

I feel fortunate to live in this middle-class neighborhood in a classy house, even by San Francisco standards. It has been renovated and modernized in all its essential parts, since I first bought it in my early twenties. It's Home Bittersweet Home, though, because it was my father's early death, when I was 19 and my inheritance at 21 that made it possible. The other thing that made it possible was one of Dad's last bits of great fatherly advice, namely to invest in real estate.

My home may be Victorian, but it's dotted with near futuristic do-dads like Cosma and Hazel. Hazel is a stout little droid in a French maid's costume. The costume was my idea, but considering the Crystal Ball, you probably already guessed I'm really into costumes.

To tell the truth, my friend, Ira the Inventor, has always been smitten with me. Before Curt was back in my life, it was awkward and more difficult to deflect Ira's affections. Still, even when I was single, I always made it clear that my feelings for him were platonic. Now he has resigned himself to worshipping me from afar, but he has never given up on delighting me with his brainchildren. He is constantly upgrading and tinkering with them, which gives him a good excuse to hang out with me. Curt thinks he's pathetic and finds him mildly annoying. I think he's sweet in a classic, nerdy way.

Hazel answered my buzz and rolled herself into the kitchen. She's an R2 unit, just like in the movies.

"Coffee, Ms. Micki?"

She was well trained, too.

"No, thanks. I was going to ask you for some, Hazel, but I'm having second thoughts. I think I'll do yoga now. Better make it later." Getting hyped isn't conducive to relaxation.

Hazel said *yes ma'am* and rolled away.

Since there wasn't a thing I could do about Foy until Hans delivered his fax and the crackpot reacted, I decided to do Stage 1 of getting ready for my big night—yoga and meditation. Getting centered. Pulling myself together for whatever I'd have to do. I needed to be in a grounded place, especially since I had no idea about what else might happen today. I knew I could trust Hans to get the fax to Foy by the deadline. I'd take a literal breather …

…but the universe refused me a moment's respite. My cell phone rang. I squeezed out a minute before faxing Foy to get out of my jammies and into my sweats—big difference. I fished the phone out of my pocket before it could irritate me with another round of tinny Bach Inventions, a far cry from the real thing, at least to my inner pianist. Reminder to myself: Find new ring tone.

"Micki … Tasha!" It was Natasha Grayson, IOPEA's second in command.

"First, I want to tell you *not* to get excited, because what I'm about to tell you is already in the process of being fixed."

I laughed. "I can hardly wait! Actually, I am amazed that we got past 8 AM on the big day without some kind of event planning disaster."

"Well, here's the thing. I called the caterer to be sure her staff remembered to use their special china with the silver trim for the hors d'oeuvres …"

"Yeah?"

" … and the woman I talked to—apparently some new hired help—

asked me why we wanted to go through all that trouble for only 30 people."

"What??? Are you serious?"

I literally grabbed my chest and felt my heart almost explode out of my chest cavity.

"Whoa, Micki, calm down. I'm telling you, it's already in the process of being fixed.

"They dropped an important zero! Where did they get the idea it was 30 not 300?"

"Well, that's the really odd part. I talked to Hedy, the owner. She told me you called and told her the turnout was way low, but you were going to go through with it anyway. She said you told her to plan for an intimate gathering of 30."

"What???" I was starting to have more whats than a floodlight.

"Micki, this was obviously someone's idea of a sick joke. Do you think that guy's behind it, the one who has been calling and sending everyone at work all those strange e-mails?"

"Bingo. You have no idea what's been going on here today. And this really has to be hush-hush. I don't want everyone worried and upset at the most exciting event in IOPEA's history—worse yet, I don't want them to stay away because of some bizarro."

I gave Tasha the scoop and swore her to secrecy.

"The important thing, Micki, is that Hedy knows it was a hoax. I suggest you call her. She feels terrible."

"More than that, I'll call her and give her a secret code or keyword, so she will know it's me from here on out, not someone pretending to be me. You know, like a PIN number at the ATM."

I called Hedy, and she apologized profusely. I could almost hear her beating her breast, chanting my mother's twist on *mea culpa* from the Latin Mass, "I am a maximum culprit."

"Look, Hedy, you didn't know." I wondered who could have done such a good job imitating me, but then, Hedy and I only talked a few times a year. It wasn't like I have the world's most distinctive voice—although some people thought so in a figurative sense. Come to think of it, my mother is the only person I know of, where people can't tell the difference between us on the phone. Nah. Loni was narcissistic, loved being the center of attention, and hated that I lived in the limelight instead of her—but she's not *that* warped. After all, she *is* my mother.

Hedy assured me that there was plenty of time to go back to the original plan for 300, since this mix-up was discovered early in the day. It would take jumping through a few hoops—not a problem because IO-PEA was one of her best customers. She'd be happy to do it, especially since she had been so—uh—gullible.

What Foy hadn't done so far in violence, he made up for in havoc. The thought of there only being food and drinks for one tenth of the people invited to the Crystal Ball made me want to scream for both its perversity and cleverness. Too bad he wasn't on our side, I thought, remembering that Darth Vader was once a good guy.

My cell phone said 8:30 AM. I gave a quick call to Hans to make sure he was making Foy's deadline. He'd already faxed him and told me a copy was on its way to me for all the sense it would make to me as a scientific civilian. Every discipline has its language, and I laughed remembering a girlfriend who asked me once, garbling astrological jargon, if her boyfriend's "Mars is conjunct my quincox."

I told Curt about the food fiasco. He was starting to get pissed about how much Foy was upsetting me. While I'd like to think it was pure empathy on his part, finally coming to the surface, I suspected it was really because: (a) I am not "in the mood" when I am upset, and (b) when I am upset long enough, I get cranky and tend to make everyone around me miserable. When I get into that place somewhere between PMS and hot flashes—the hormonal midpoint between my biological and actual age—he couldn't even take comfort and guy-bond with Thusie, because he's allergic to him.

"When you're done standing on your head, chanting Om, or whatever you have to do for yourself next, we have to talk."

"About what?"

"About a plan to disarm this guy. He's starting to be a pain... a pest. Two can play that game."

I shuddered to think of how big a pain Curt could be if he really put his mind to it.

But I let it drop for the moment to take care of myself. I meandered into the living room and pulled my yoga props out of their basket in the corner—mat, blocks, and strap. I selected a Rodney Yee DVD that started out in my favorite position—Shavasana or corpse pose, which I realize, is ironic for an immortalist. It's supposedly one of the hardest asanas or poses, because it requires total relaxation. You can tell yoga comes from the East. Only in America and other parts of the hyperactive Western world would stillness be that difficult. Especially after a couple of cups of leaded.

The session ended with plenty of zither music and time to meditate. I focused on affirmations, and said to myself in my mind:

"I, Micki, will be a great leader today. I will rise to the occasion of whatever is called for."

"I, Micki, am fearless and know exactly what to do and when to do it."

"I, Micki, am serene and centered, regardless of whatever happens around me."

The doorbell rang. It startled me so much; I almost levitated as I jerked in simple crossed-legs pose.

No sooner did the ding dong than my tubby little Hazel rolled by, headed to the front door. In a gleeful tone, almost nauseating to a non-morning person, she announced, "Doorbell, Ms. Micki."

"A droid with a profound sense of the obvious," I commented to Thusie, who was now rubbing against my knee and meowing hysterically for his canned food. "Hazel will help you in a minute," I promised.

Hazel Hot Wheels, Curt's pet name for my loopy little helper, raised her arm to the peephole in the door. A whirring sound accompanied an elongation of her "index finger," which Hazel screwed into the viewer. Within a few blips, a sound that reminded me of an old coffee percolator, Hazel had assimilated the visual image and matched it to a programmed file. This particular face was high on the Close Friend and Relative List.

"Ms. Tansy," she said. I unknotted my legs and sprang up in alarm.

"Ms. April, too."

I nearly ran Hazel off the road in the foyer, double-checking the peephole to make sure she got it right and that it wasn't some relative look-alike, just like my voice-alike that nearly screwed up the catering.

I almost yanked the handle off the door opening it.

"What are you doing here? Why did you leave the house after I warned you to stay ..."

"Wait a minute, Micki," April complained. "You said don't let Tansy out of my sight. She's in my sight. You didn't say we were under house arrest."

"God, you are so literal. Are you sure you're really related to this family?"

The rest of us played the symbols. April was so verbatim. It had to be her mother's genes, because this sort of concrete interpretation of words was definitely not a Michaels characteristic.

"Look, we got bored," April said. "None of Curt's friends showed up yet, and we were curious about what's going on. And hungry. I didn't have a thing in the house."

"Yeah, let's eat!" Tansy said eagerly, holding up two bags from O'Berger's.

Dread hit me like a tidal wave. I was about to drown in yet another ominous psychic impression. What happened to the Micki of yesterday? A person so positive, someone I know once accused me of being *upbeat and glossy*?

"Tansy," I barked. "I don't want you to touch that food till Curt looks at it. Come on," I said, running into the kitchen and motioning her and her mom to follow.

"What's all the commotion?" Curt asked. "I see you two escaped."

"That's just it," I said, grabbing the bags from Tansy and holding them as far out in front of me as my arms could stretch, as if they stank any worse than most fast food.

They're being watched—followed. How do we know Foy didn't get to someone at O'Berger's, someone who tampered with their food? Tansy is a regular. She hits O'Berger's almost every time she comes here, on her way over. Foy could have pre-arranged something for her next stop and activated his plan, once he saw April and Tansy headed there."

Curt sighed a long, slow one—the full length of his six-foot, one-inch still hot body. I liked the way the light played off his gray hair. When I looked at him with love eyes, he bore an uncanny resemblance to Richard Gere in *An Officer and a Gentleman*. A small part of me wished he'd carry me off, remembering that romantic scene from the movie, away from all my responsibilities. I wondered what it would be liked to be rescued—just long enough to catch my breath.

He was quiet for way too long. When he finally spoke, he said, "Michele, I think you're starting to go paranoid on me."

His blue-green eyes were moist with concern.

I started bawling. He gathered me into a hug. Tansy tried to seize the moment and went for the bags on the table behind us, but I busted her—caught her out of my peripheral vision and grabbed her arm.

After the minor freak-out, I did more Pranayama—deep breathing—and begged them all to listen to me.

"When I get these feelings, they are rarely wrong. So raid the refrigerator and leave the O'Bergers alone till we can check them out. So we end up trashing breakfast. The worst you lose is a few bucks, April. I'll pay you back."

Tansy looked at April. April looked at Tansy. They looked at me in stereo, like I had a screw loose. They raised their eyes toward heaven for help—a caricature of one another. They ran to the fridge and started stuffing their faces, standing there with the door open.

They were absolute cookie cutter images, a mother-daughter matched set of repetitious mannerisms. Even though they shared both my Greek and Slovakian genes, at times like this, our peasant ancestry from Kysta dominated. I could see the ancestral village with six houses and an out-house, thatched roofs and straw to warm the dirt floor in winter. If we could go back in a time machine, two centuries, they'd be strong like bulls, needing lots of food to plow fields. The modern refrigerator would be out of place, but not the feeding frenzy.

Back to the future, Curt humored me. He picked up the O'Berger's bags and listened to them.

"Nothing ticking." He headed out the kitchen door to the garden behind the house and our city patio. I knew he'd be combining further examination of the food with sneaking a smoke, which I did not allow in the house.

"Why don't you two get some plates and sit down and eat, you know, like a couple of regular human beings with manners." April glared at me. Tansy grinned, a half-eaten cigarillo of string cheese hanging from the side of her mouth. She looked like she ought to be banished to the patio with Curt.

Instead, I went out and joined him, fanning smoke downwind from my face.

"Doesn't look strange, act strange, or smell strange," Curt declared about the bags of food.

"Let me get one of the lab type guys from IOPEA to look at it. One of our members —a guy named Marty—used to be a crime scene investigator, and he has an unbelievable lab in his basement and connections to anything else he might need to analyze it.

"You've got ex-cops in that organization?"

"You'd be surprised who we've got, Curt. How 'bout that? People who were once just like you."

His eyes narrowed. "Well, if you don't mind looking like a fool in front of your friend when you send him on a wild goose chase, why should I care?"

"Meanwhile, let's put this stuff somewhere that Thusie can't get at, till I can call this guy.

The mother-daughter munch-a-thon was already on Mile 2. Both of them were digging into a pile of toast. Neither of them asked what happened to Tansy's O'Bean or April's O'Berger. Either sounded disgusting to me as breakfast. Their taste buds were having a new affair with toast and jam, and they were oblivious to my worries.

"What if the food was tampered with?" Curt wondered aloud. "How would they have done that?"

"I'm not sure, but if you want to be really helpful, you could call one of your cop friends while I call mine—see if there was any kind of incident reported at the O'Berger's they were at. Foy or his guys could have seen them going in and grabbed an employee and the bag ... you know, and did something to it."

"That sounds really unlikely, but if it'll put your mind at ease so you can enjoy the rest of your big day, I'll call."

"April, did you go to your usual O'Berger's?

"Yeah, Fillmore."

"I'm on it," Curt said, and we went to our respective corners of the kitchen with our cell phones to make our calls.

After I hung up, April picked up their dishes, but not the crumbs, and asked what they should do now. I stalled to hear what Curt might think about that.

"I had a call waiting while I was talking to Ace Elliot, my ex-cop friend. Mary Beth Boniface called back. She's that former FBI agent I mentioned who retired here in SF. Has family here. She'll be happy to watch the girls, as long as they don't have to hang at April's like sitting ducks. Mary Beth thinks moving will keep Foy and anyone who might be working for him diverted and keep them diverted in a have-fun kind of way. I told her we'd give them money to go to the mall."

"How does that sound?" I asked April and Tansy.

"Great!" they said as one.

"Mary Beth doesn't live far. Says she can be here in 15-20 minutes from whenever I say the word. She'll call in every couple of hours to check in. But first, I have to figure out an escape route."

"I don't get it."

"The only way in and out of our place is by the front door or from the side of the house through the back door and patio area. It's not like we've got a handy alley for pick-up. The street in front of the house is the only way to leave to go anywhere, and it's completely visible. Before the kids walk out to meet Mary Beth, I have to be sure Foy hasn't got surveillance on us."

Good point. San Francisco alleys existed, but we didn't have one. Houses were cheek by jowl as my mother, Loni, liked to say. They often backed up and sidled up to each other.

Curt hurried to the bay window in the front of the house and emitted a loud expletive. He ran back to the kitchen and told us why.

"There's a black sedan. Two guys. That means I have to stage a diversion."

Curt paced a few times, deepening the line between his eyebrows.

"OK, how 'bout this? I get Mary Beth to pull up and ask the guys directions. While they're diverted talking to her, you girls come out the back of the house, up the side of it, and crawl into the back seat of Micki's Prius, parked in the driveway. I drive you to a meet-up point with Mary Beth a few blocks away. But you girls have to act calm, cool, and collected. No nervous moves, no talking, just go for the back seat very quietly, close the door, and duck your heads down."

"Is this safe?" I asked.

"Yeah, it's fine," Curt answered, already speed dialing Mary Beth.

I gave the go-ahead, knowing that Curt would never entrust the loves of my life to anyone who didn't know what she was doing. I promised my brother on his deathbed that I'd always watch over his family—our family.

Next thing I knew, Curt was completely busting up in conversation with Mary Beth.

"You can't be serious. In this neighborhood? We may as well meet at

O'Berger's. Hide things right out in the open. At least there's parking."

I wondered what he meant about our neighborhood. I was in the dark again, hearing only his side of Curt's conversation.

"It's all set," Curt said. "She'll be here in 15 and will call when she's about a minute away. We'll be poised with April and Tansy at the back door. Micki, you watch the front window, and when you see MB pull up, yell 'go!'"

In what seemed like an eye blink, I saw—and heard—Mary Beth's new, silver Corvette squeal to a stop parallel with the black sedan. What is it with retired FBI agents and luxury sports cars? They must time retirement with their midlife crisis. Curt had an Alfa Romeo Spider convertible. That's why his car's in the garage and mine's in the driveway.

I gave my verbal green light for Curt and the girls to spring into action. Then I watched sideways, perpendicular to the wall, so I couldn't be seen peering out the bay window. It had a direct line of sight from the other side of the street. April and Tansy were quiet as church mice. I couldn't say the same thing for Mary Beth.

I had cracked one of the windows, so I could hear what was happening on the street. Loud catcalls were emanating from the black car and besides the whistling, a lot of "whoa!" and laughter. Mary Beth had created a commotion while Curt backed out of the driveway.

I couldn't wait till Curt came back from swapping the girls with Mary Beth to hear what the noise was all about.

"She asked for more than directions," Curt said. "She lifted up her shirt, showed 'em her goodies, and asked if they wanted to buy. The conversation and chaos that followed bought us more time."

"But there's a young girl involved in this!" I protested, thinking of Tansy's impressionable age.

"The girls couldn't even see her. They were scrunched down in the back seat of your car. Mary Beth was making sure the goons were too busy looking at something else to be following what was going on in the driveway. We were quick. I'll bet they never even saw the girls get in … probably figured I was running to the store."

While I let everything sink in, I mused on the irony of this day.

I couldn't believe my friends Meg O'Malley and Joel Berger were playing a roundabout part in this increasingly odd drama. Years ago, I'd teased them about starting a fast food chain, insisting they should call it Berger's Burgers. This was mostly to rib Megan, a strict vegetarian.

But one idea led to another, and Meg and Joel decided to make their marriage of opposites really work for them—Irish woman, Jewish man, a vegetarian and a beefeater.

They capitalized on blending their differences, and that's how O'Berger's was born. Veggie burgers, turkey burgers, bean burgers, hamburgers, and a Big O' in the Sky. In their logo in neon, the O was a bagel—one choice of bread at O'Berger's—the apostrophe, a shamrock. They gave me hope that maybe—just maybe—Curt and I could be just as creative in blending our differences into something as wildly successful.

Some days I'd even settle for a good sandwich.

Chapter 5

Tansy and April went merrily on their way to the Stonestown Galleria with Mary Beth, who was nearly positive that she and Curt had managed to give Foy's cronies the slip. I doubted Foy would do his own dirty work, so I figured the thugs in the black sedan were creeps in cahoots with him.

April and Tansy were apparently getting a big bang out of the intrigue, according to Mary Beth's early first report. I was hoping this would be the only kind of bang we had to deal with all day—except for maybe the bedroom fireworks kind with Curt at some point.

Speaking of Curt, I was so grateful to him for finding someone to keep my nieces in tow and occupied while we dealt with the rest of the day's events. He had just hung up with Mary Beth and told me what she said.

"You know, Curt Stern, you are a lot nicer guy than you let on."

"Don't let it get around. I have my image to think about."

My cell phone rang. It was Marty. His preliminary test showed that the O'Bergers were not just full of beef and beans, but something that would have put April and Tansy to sleep for a long time.

"Cyanide?" I gasped.

"Something more like truth serum," Marty said. "It wouldn't have killed either one of them, but it sure would have sent them night-night for awhile, and God only knows what they might have talked about in their sleep."

"Guess Foy was hoping for some inside scoop on my life or IOPEA. He must be desperate, because my nieces know next to nothing about what I do. He'd be better off drugging a board member—me, for instance."

Holding April and Tansy hostage to encourage me to talk—that made sense from a criminal point of view. Foy was smart in some ways but his logic was lacking in others. Maybe if I could keep noting his weaknesses, I could find a way to exploit them. Normally, I'm looking to avoid hurting people in their soft spots, but Foy was threatening those dearest to me. He was bringing out a side of me I hardly knew I had.

I thanked Marty profusely for his work on the O'Bergers, swore him to silence, and hung up shaking my head. Before I could even tell him what Marty said, Curt's cell phone rang. My bet was on Ace for the caller, but I couldn't really tell what Ace Elliott had come up with from Curt's side of the conversation. Curt was doing the face-change thing as he hung up.

He shook his head.

"I don't believe it."

"What?" I demanded to know.

"There was an incident at the Fillmore O'Berger's, all right."

"I figured from what Marty found, but you go first."

"Some monkey thumped a guy, dragged and left this young kid half-naked in the men's room. The perp apparently put on the kid's uniform."

I picked up the story based on what Marty had told me, piecing it together as I talked and shared it with Curt.

"And while Foy or his flunky was dressed like an O'Berger flipper, he slipped some truth serum into April and Tansy's patties. Injected it probably, Marty said."

"You have to be kidding me." Curt scratched his head, displaying his own nervous tic.

"I wish I were. Want to tell me again, how I shouldn't worry about this guy? I don't want to think of what he might have done to them while they were under, although Marty's pretty sure he—or they—just wanted to get information out of them. If he had other motives, he could have just used a sedative."

"He's getting to be a pretty serious pain in the ass, Micki, I'll give you that."

"I don't know what to do … where to go from here. So far, the only person who has really been able to thumb her nose at Foy is Mary Beth."

Despite my initial outrage, I had gotten quite a vicarious thrill out of the simple way she outsmarted Foy's Frick and Frack lookouts. She almost blew them a kiss—she was lucky and audacious!—as Curt stole two of his surveillance subjects right out from under their noses.

"There's still been no bodily harm done. If you can just keep cool, I think we can come up with a plan to keep him out of your hair at the party. Then you'll be a happy do-gooder and I'll be happily retired for yet another day."

I stared at him, unsure if he really minded helping me. I decided to give him the benefit of the doubt.

"I need to calm myself—take some flower essences—meditate. I need a little time, Curt. You know how this works for me—from the inside out. Think about it for awhile, while I take care of myself, and let's meet back here in the kitchen in a half-hour or forty-five minutes to consider our options."

Curt agreed, and I headed off …

MY MEDITATION WAS DEEP and mind-altering. I could almost feel the circuitry of my brain slow down and rewire itself into what's often described as the calm at the center of a hurricane. Every atom of my being felt washed with a balm of white light, a strong emanation of my own energy field I could see behind my eyelids, even with my eyes closed and the room darkened. I took three deep breaths to come out of my altered state. I felt powerful and grounded.

I headed for my home office and one of my favorite pieces of furniture—an antique mahogany dentist's cabinet with row upon row of tiny wooden drawers. They held my complete stash of flower remedies, over 500 bottles.

With the battle of guns and roses in full bloom, I couldn't help but remember the first time I explained to Curt what they are and how they work.

"They're tinctures of flower petals. The flower petals are floated in spring water and set out in the sun like making sun tea."

"What the …" He couldn't even evoke his most versatile expletive for laughing out loud. When he could compose himself just a little, he asked, "And this does exactly what?"

"Each flower changes the vibration of an emotional pattern from negative to positive. For example, you always tell me I'm a worrywart. The remedy for that is Mimulus. It calms worry."

"Well, you'd better give me some of that one, because I'm worried you have lost it."

"These work at a very subtle level, Curt. They're gentler than drugs, and they have no known adverse interactions with them. They were discovered by a bacteriologist turned homeopathic physician during World War I. They were first used to combat shell shock in battle."

"Do you drink the petals?"

"No need. The vibrations are there. Take out the petals, mix with a little brandy for preservative, and then take them under the tongue like a homeopathic remedy, a few drops at a time, usually four times a day."

"Well, I guess if nothing else, the brandy will make you feel better."

I told him it sometimes takes three to four weeks for the shift to occur, which he considered nearly useless. While the effects can occasionally be immediate, I didn't want to be like one of those diet ads with an asterisk and fine print, admitting these results were unusual.

I didn't bother with my favorite part of the spiel, how people have always known intuitively that flowers belong at every major human turning point: birth, death, marriage, and every occasion of high emotions for celebrating love and life in-between. I knew this subtlety would be lost on Curt.

Now I had to come up with a blend to help me save the day. Even though I only had hours for it to take effect, after years as a certified essence practitioner and avid taker of the remedies, they could shift my energy in hours, sometimes minutes. Mimulus was a given. I added Larch for cheerful leadership, Trumpet Vine for dynamic speech and communication, since I'd be making a major address at the Ball. Queen Anne's Lace was for higher sight and wisdom, which I would need with Foy on my tail. Last but not least, I rounded it off with Golden Yarrow to keep me feeling surrounded by a protective bubble of light from the high vibrations of the crowd and any new craziness Foy might dish out. To know what to do, I had to open my sensitivities, but to stand in front of God and everyone without some filters would be like hiking the Sahara without sunscreen.

After taking the drops, I headed for my yoga sling, one of those contraptions that look like an indoor version of a kid's playground swing. It has a corduroy seat, suspended by straps of nylon webbing from the ceiling. You lie on your stomach, and then work yourself down to the floor, till you're propped by your hands on the floor with your head hanging between them. The trick is to wiggle the seat down to your upper thighs. Once you do, it's easy to hang there comfortably, upside down, to replicate the effects of headstand in yoga, without your head actually touching the floor. I'm fairly limber, but I'm not talented at standing on my head, except in a figurative way. For friends, loved ones, or a passionate cause, I would bend over backwards, but headstand requires the neck muscles of a bull.

Once the blood went rushing to my head, it cleared away the last cobwebs of worry—maybe with a little help from the Mimulus. However, an image appeared that was as real as if the person in it were standing in front of me, while I mused at how funny she looked upside-down. It was Virginia, our accountant at IOPEA. Even with no sound or a volume knob for my psychic impression, I could tell she was screaming.

"Virginia Goody, Ace Accountant,
Never a hair or a decimal point
out of place."

~ From a poem by Micki Michaels

Chapter 6

S o much for my late morning date with Curt to strategize about Foy.

My poem about Virginia sped through my head with the wind in my hair in Curt's top-down Spider. His Alfa Romeo sports car is roughly the color of a Yellow Cab. As far as I can tell, it's the only flashy thing about him.

Spidey's a pipsqueak version of the yellow 'Cuda convertible driven by San Francisco's famous fictional cop, Nash Bridges, in my all-time favorite TV show of the same name. We jumped a hump ascending California Street, taking the wave of pavement like a renegade speedboat. Remembering Nash only added melancholy to abject fear, as it triggered mourning for my favorite canceled show. Mourning fit the moment. I was scared to death for what we might find … if I didn't freeze to death first! After living through so many extreme East Coast winters, Curt figured it was nearly summer when the temperature pushed 50 degrees.

We lived ten minutes or less, depending on traffic, from my office at IOPEA. It was a weekday, so it was business as usual pre-holiday. Some people would be getting off early at noon. The brisk air was sobering and hair-raising in a literal way.

Once we hit Presidio Avenue, there were frustrating stop signs almost every block till we got to the entrance of the Presidio itself, the old army post turned urban reuse project. We hugged the curvy road under the dark canopy of century-old eucalyptus, cypress and pine trees. The scent of pine dominated. It made me remember that Pine was one of the first flower essences I ever took—for guilt. Once a Catholic ... Soon we were skidding to a stop in front of IOPEA headquarters. For over 200 years, the Presidio served as an army post. IOPEA was lucky to be one of the tenants in more than 250 buildings, most of them historic, in a beautiful park setting in a place of national significance.

My mind, on the other hand, was in a not-so-pretty place. Images of deranged and creepy critters from every horror film I'd ever seen were behind the door, in my imagination, as Curt and I pushed it open to enter IOPEA headquarters. It was unlocked, just like we were afraid we'd find it. IOPEA had a burglar alarm compatible with the Presidio's requirements. How this could happen was a mystery to me, unless the last person out failed to activate the alarm.

That would have been me.

I thought I remembered setting it, but I didn't have time to doubt myself over how we got into this fine mess. I needed to stay focused on finding out how bad it was and what we should do about it.

Curt ran ahead of me, drawn gun first at arm's length, doing that dance you see in every police show, where the hero expects to find an armed bad guy around every corner. He had to be ready to duck; aim, fire or spring—whatever was needed. I followed a respectful distance behind, judging how far to hold back by the wildness of Curt's gestures. Since I thrive on order, not even my worst nightmares and horror film flashbacks prepared me for the mess I saw.

"I guess this is what they call ransacked."

Papers, files, and office supplies were thrown everywhere. Desk drawers were open and the offices, cubicles, and hallways looked like the aftermath of a tornado. Every computer in the place was on; most of them open to their hard drive directory, revealing the name, date created, and size of every file. The sight was enough to make a neatnik gag. In fact, since my flair for order was nothing compared to hers, I tried to convince myself that Virginia couldn't possibly be here, intuitive vision aside, or she would have already tidied up. I knew I was just trying to make myself feel better. I walked through the hall like a bulldog, faced each cube, and drank in the bad news. I kept preparing myself for the possibility of finding her somewhere—hurt—or God forbid ...

My trembling hands went to my head on reflex, fingers pulling back handfuls of auburn hair. Somehow, focusing on the chaos allowed me a few moments' relief from concern about Virginia, someone I cared about.

"How will I even begin to do damage control on this mess?" I moaned.

Once we were relatively sure there were no bad guys or broken accountants in the main office area, I ran ahead.

"Will you let me go first?" Curt yelled. Oh yeah, I forgot. I had James Bond with me. Deferring to the guy in my life, even with a good excuse, was new to me.

"After you, Double-Oh-Seven," I said, bowing at the waist in a kowtow complete with hand flourish.

"You won't be such a smart ass if someone armed is on the other side of this door."

I didn't bother to one-up him. We stormed the lunchroom. Mean-spirited mayhem was the new decorating scheme. Someone had emptied the fridge and flung everything liquid, solid, and in-between haphazardly into the room from floor to ceiling. Broken bottles, empty containers, and a cacophony of mismatched smells splattered the canvas of the scene. There was even leftover pasta on the wall, giving me two seconds of comic relief in memory of the classic moment in the movie, *The Odd Couple*, where slobby Oscar throws linguine on the wall, to the horror of Felix the fussbudget. Some of the long-forgotten food in the sortie had reached the point of science experiments. I started gagging, but before I could make the situation even more wretched, I heard a muffled sound coming from the bathroom on the far side of the room.

"I hear something!" I said to Curt, too loudly for someone standing right next to me. He screwed his pointer finger into the offended ear.

I bee-lined for the restroom. Curt ran after me. I rattled the handle, but it was locked from the inside.

He put his ear to the door. "From the sound of it, she's gagged. Probably bound. They must have pushed the button on the way out to just to make it harder to get to her once she was discovered. Nice guys. At least they're consistent. Nasty all the way."

"The bastards! If it weren't for my intuition, no one would have discovered her till we came back to work on January 2nd. We've got to break the door down!"

"Get out of the way," Curt commanded, pushing me aside in a way that felt rude but vital.

I was stunned when he shot off the knob, not even stopping to consider less damaging alternatives. Funny, I just noticed I hadn't even been outraged when I first noticed he was carrying a weapon. I wondered about myself for a second. A gun seemed so normal in this fiasco; I never even stopped to ask him if it was necessary. I shuddered at what any of the board members— much less regular members—of IOPEA would think of what was going on here at Longevity Central, where ecology, health, love, and peace were supposed to reign. What was happening to me?

There before us was Virginia Goody, Ace Accountant—just as Curt predicted—bound and gagged. There were bruises on one side of her face. Her eyes were crazed, her muffled cries were now much louder, and her hair—and a few other things—were very out of place. Someone had ripped open her white blouse, cut her left bra strap, and cut her on the breast just over her heart. The cut was not deep; it was the symbolism and the instant, obvious visual that she had been tortured or tormented into believing the intruders would stab her to death. I felt a wave in my gut of combined outrage, empathy, and responsibility—a nauseating disorientation familiar from the Loma Prieta Earthquake of '89, when I was suddenly shooting the curl on dry land with no surfboard.

Curt had the wherewithal to roll the chair out of the confined space before he began cutting her bonds behind her back with the scissors he found on the bathroom floor. I looked into Virginia's darting eyes, and I touched the side of her face before loosening the knot in the gag.

I have never heard such a stream of profanity roll from the lips of a prissy woman with a virginal name. Someone had unleashed Virginia's inner demons, and her head all but spun around, *Exorcist* style, as she frothed angry venom—first at Curt, then her tormentors. "Pistol whipped," she spat out toward the end of the tirade.

"You sonofabitch! You could have shot me to death. What the hell do you think you're doing, shooting off a lock with someone right on the other side of the door?"

I rubbed her shoulders, safely behind her.

"I can only imagine how a gunshot must have sounded at close range after all you've been through," I said so softly; I nearly whispered.

Virginia had no notion it was Curt on the other side of the door and that he knew what he was doing. I wasn't about to take away from the bigger issue of her trauma by defending him.

After the first raid in her war of words, Virginia swore more at the absent perpetrators, and then burst into an explosion of tears, pent-up pressure spewing water like a hydrant on a hot summer day. Only I did not feel refreshed.

I ran back to my office to get her some Emergency Remedy. I had only glanced around the room in my previous assessment of the wreckage, figuring my desk and surroundings were a carbon copy of everyone else's. I plunked myself down into my high-backed, ergonomic chair at my circular, oak desk ... and while groping in my junk drawer for the flower essences, I saw it. I shuddered. I screamed.

Someone had ripped Tansy's photo from the frame on my desk and stabbed it onto the blotter with a knife. The warning was stark enough, but it was where they stabbed the picture that curdled my blood to ice. It was a picture of her sitting in the crook of a tree, and the point of the knife was driven straight through her heart. I screamed over and over again. I hadn't stopped when Curt and Virginia ran through the door.

I drank the Emergency Remedy.

Chapter 7

Virginia grabbed the Emergency Remedy out of my hand and glugged some down right after me. She sighed, swooned a little, but recaptured most of her teetering composure. Soon she was behind my chair, efficient as ever, massaging my shoulders, a complete role reversal from just a few minutes ago. I tried to gather my wits. The flower essences began to take hold, but I still felt like I'd been run over by a semi. Until I got my next Mary Beth Report on the status of my nieces, I'd be a wreck, even if the shock had started to wear off a little.

Foy certainly knew how to make a point.

Curt was already dialing Mary Beth—right after he spewed a volcanic eruption of expletives that outdid Virginia's recent swearing-in ceremony. I had to admit; the only natural reaction to what was going on here was to curse—a lot. Gee *whiz* or *darn* wouldn't begin to express it. This was especially true, considering the typical language of an ex-FBI agent and the words of a woman who had been damming her swearing since the day she first heard a four-letter word.

"Hi, MB. Things are heating up. We're at IOPEA headquarters. Yeah, looks like this guy means business. It's clear he's targeting Tansy. I'll tell you the particulars later. Uh huh. No, I'll tell her. Have you made those guys tailing you again? Micki's beside herself. You'll have to up your reports to once an hour, maybe even every half. Yeah, sorry. No, I get it. OK." Curt looked at his watch. "If you haven't heard from me by then, call me in an hour. Yeah, 12:30. We'll be tied up here for a bit."

"What?" I hate not hearing the other side of a conversation. Tied up would not have been my choice of words.

"Tansy wanted to know her spending limit on your credit card. I said you'd call back."

"That's it?"

"You're lucky that's it. No tails on them, as far as Mary Beth can tell. April's happy to be off work on New Year's Eve, hanging out with another nice woman, and Tansy's having a ball spending your money."

Considering it was the only ball she might get today, I didn't care if she was spending my money. I was glad she was in one piece, able to do it. In fact, I didn't give a rip if she shopped till my plastic melted.

In fact, if I'd have been closer to home and had a minute to myself, I'd have ducked into St. Dominic's to light a candle and say a prayer. For now, I'd just do the short version in my mind. *Thank God!*

As tempted as I was to say "I told you so" about Foy and his danger potential, Curt was being so helpful; I didn't want to rub his nose in it. This was not a day for our childish battles about who was right. It was a day to join forces.

"Curt, I need to talk to Virginia alone for awhile. Can you make the police report?"

"Done."

"Be sure they understand—no media. Treat this like a simple burglary. Explain the sensitivities about our event."

"I have friends at SFPD."

"That's why I want you to call."

"But you realize, Micki, that this was, in fact, an assault with a deadly weapon—two of them, actually—the pistol and scissors … which reminds me that I shouldn't have touched the scissors, because they may have fingerprints!"

"They'll just take yours for an elimination sample."

I watch all the CSIs.

"Assaults with a deadly are severely punished under California law. The guy could get up to four years and fines. Worse if it's deemed a second-degree attempted murder rap, which typically brings five to nine. You may be missing your chance to get this guy out of your hair for a long time, if not for good."

I had forgotten in the heat of the moment, that Curt went to law school before he joined the FBI—in California. He lived and did one of his first gigs with the Bureau in San Francisco. I had no idea he was here at the time. He was married to someone else then, so it's just as well. Remembering that fact sent a wave of anger from my gut to the top of my head, which felt ready to explode. Curt could never commit to me, yet he married someone else and was with her for more than a decade before they divorced.

I had no time to blow my top over our past. I had to pull myself together.

"I'll leave it up to you, how you characterize what happened here. It's up to the discretion of you and your friends—however you see fit, as long as it doesn't leak to the press. Remember, Curt, I'm a peacemaker at heart, and in case this guy is just mentally imbalanced, I don't want to kill a flea with a cannon."

Even though I hate fleas.

Curt shook his head, left my office, and headed toward the reception area. After a deep breath, I morphed into Executive Mama Bear and asked Virginia how she was doing.

She bawled.

We hugged.

"I thought so. Look Virginia, I want you to take a minimum of two weeks' sick leave, more if you need it. That's what it's for. I'm going to hook you up with one of our best therapists who belongs to IOPEA. She's near Monterey. We'll send you on a retreat away from the City, as soon as the police will let you leave town. Maybe at Asilomar or Esalen, away from all this insanity."

Missing the Crystal Ball wasn't an issue for Virginia, because she wouldn't have gone, anyway, even if her hair and decimals weren't fly-ing in the wind. Her bruised face wouldn't be a deterrent, either. Fact is, she'd never be caught dead, pardon the expression, doing anything as undignified as wearing a costume, much less hanging loose in some of our playful games and eclectic spiritual ceremonies. At least if the worst had happened today, she'd have been in full accountant regalia, shoes shined and suit crisply dry cleaned at the earth-friendly cleaners. It wasn't difficult to guess her Virgo Sun sign. It matched her virginal name and her kinship with similar fictional characters, such as Felix Unger and Monk, the defective detective.

Here's the part where I'm embarrassed to admit that I'm a Virgo, too—in case you haven't guessed by my overactive gag reflexes around messes. At least I like to think I've evolved past which bathroom bowl cleaner to use and onto doing my part to save the world from going down the toilet.

"What about Sniffles."

Virginia has a cat, I kid you not, with chronic allergies. I call him Snot Rag behind her back.

"You're welcome to leave Sno—I mean Sniff with me. He and Thusie got along great when you brought him over that one time."

Never mind that time was B.C.—Before Curt lived with me—and Curt's allergic. This was an emergency, and she didn't need to know that we'd be calling Curt Sniffles before it was all over. I'd think of something. There was a flower essence for oversensitivity, if he'd just take it…

I dialed Dr. Nancy Marietta from my desk phone and actually reached her on the first try. In the middle of our conversation, the other line blinked, and I had one of those feelings. I begged off and told Nancy I'd call her back.

"Ms. Michaels, I hope you're enjoying our remodel of your headquar-ters."

Foy! I covered the mouthpiece and whispered to Virginia, "Tell Curt the bad guy is on my Line 2." Then I made the shoosh sign with my index finger over my lips. I knew she'd explain to him how to listen in from the front desk.

"I hope you got my message about your niece, Ms. Michaels. And by the way, I hope she's enjoyin' herself, she is, at the Stonestown Galleria with her mother and that FBI lady."

"How ...?"

Foy cut me off. "How I know things is none of your business, Ms. Michaels. Your business is to give me the secret of long life, and if the formula your man sent me earlier does not do that ... well, I think you would be gettin' the picture."

Foy cut off just as Curt cut in. I ran out to meet him at Reception. He and Virginia stared at me in tandem. Curt blurted out, "What did he say?"

"He knows the girls are at the mall. I don't know how he knows."

"Shit," Curt said.

That just about summed it up.

Chapter 8

Curt had just hung up with his Ace in the hole, Ace Elliott that is, his friend who recently retired from the SFPD. Curt called in the burglary and malicious mischief at IOPEA—and downplayed the assault, which he didn't characterize as a possible murder attempt. I hated being less than forthright with the cops about what happened. I talked myself into believing that the pistol whipping and scissor snip near Virginia's heart were only scare tactics, however traumatizing they were to her. I did not want to escalate this mess; I wanted to contain it from going any crazier.

In my heart, I doubted it was a murder attempt, though I couldn't argue that Foy or his agent had assaulted Virginia with potentially deadly weapons. I didn't have much experience with guns. However, given some bad haircuts I've had in my day, I knew the full-range of how scissors could be murder.

I reasoned Foy wouldn't get enough mileage out of killing Virginia. From what little I could piece together about Foy, even though I hated to think in these cold terms, Virginia would be chump change in the stakes Foy was playing for. It would hurt me—and IOPEA—to lose a staff member, but he must have figured he'd have to hit closer to home in order to get the so-called secret. Somehow, he seemed to know that my nieces were like daughters to me, and he chose the younger of the mother/daughter duo, the one who was more vulnerable—as if he knew I had made a deathbed promise to my brother to take care of them.

That idea gave me the creeps, almost as if this guy could read my mind—or had been talking to my blabbermouth mother. I wasn't sure which one would be worse.

I knew Curt could finesse these things and help send downwind the stink of a good story in case National Tell-All or any of the other gossip rags picked it up on the police band. All I would need is the headline, *Attempted Murder at Longevity International.* Great for business.

Curt dialed Mary Beth immediately.

"MB, get April and Tansy to the nearest police station ASAP. I think Foy has them bugged. He knows you're there. He called Micki and mentioned the mall. Ask the mall guard to walk you to your car, and if he won't, call me back. I'll get you."

I would have figured Foy just made a lucky guess on where any 13-year-old would hide out, if he hadn't identified the mall by name.

A few beats later, I heard more of Curt's one-way conversation and intelligence know-how in action.

"Yeah, work with them to look at Tansy's cell phone, purse, and person. Somehow, they must have planted it, probably at O'Berger's. We'll figure out the why and wherefores later. I'll meet you at Taraval. Yeah, that's the closest police station to the mall, right? They won't follow you to the cops. And if we can de-bug her, maybe the rest of Micki's big day will go smoothly."

From your mouth to God's ear, I thought. The day was more than half-gone. There was so much to get ready. How was I supposed to be a fully dressed, calm and collected leader by 7:30 tonight when the first people started arriving at the Ball?

I'd have a better chance finding a dozen eligible bachelors in San Francisco that weren't gay.

I wanted to flee with Curt to be with the kids. Only because of his deep connections to the SFPD would either of us be allowed to leave the scene, and after brief questioning, to stay in touch by phone. I couldn't leave Virginia alone, though, in her diminished state with her hair and her decimals flying all over the place, facing a grilling with the cops without support. I didn't think till much later about the implications of this incident, how she might go permanently haywire because of it—that we could possibly lose the best accountant IOPEA could ever find. She managed our books in a way that kept our nonprofit easily afloat, while never crossing the line of making any real money.

I called Tasha. She agreed to meet Virginia at IOPEA and stay with her till the cops released her. She'd take her home and talk with Nancy Marietta about getting Virginia to Monterey County. Assuming the cops would let her leave San Francisco—likely given Curt's connections—Tasha would gather up Virginia's Kleenex cat and all his kitty gear and take him to my house. Tasha was living on a temporary basis, between apartments, with her daughter Darcy. Darcy had a dog, so Sniffles had to go to my house early. Darcy didn't mind Virginia staying with them for a day or two till the holiday was over and Tasha could drive our addled accountant to her retreat. Since Darcy wasn't into IOPEA, she didn't mind baby-sitting Virginia while Tasha attended the Crystal Ball.

Those arrangements made, we'd head for the Taraval neighborhood police station near the mall, leaving the rest of the inspection of the crime scene up to Curt's cop friends. We knew we'd be hearing from them. Even though Mary Beth had the situation under control for now, I couldn't wait to see April and Tansy at Taraval with my own eyes, which were still spinning.

I was so alarmed for April and Tansy's safety; I didn't even think about the damage Tansy might have already done to my credit line, which knowing her, was probably considerable, since she had asked how far she could go.

I was wondering the same thing about Foy—how far he'd go to get something I couldn't deliver.

At least, so far, Foy hadn't questioned the authenticity of Hans's formula. I could only assume he still thought it was for real. If only! This day was likely to age me ten years. Forget flower essences. If it were the real McCoy, I'd swallow a whole bottle of Hans's youth tonic.

By the time we got to Taraval Station, Mary Beth and the local boys in blue had ferreted out the bug in Tansy's cell phone. Clever. Anyone knows a young girl and her cell phone are never parted, and the chip allowed Foy and his cronies to follow Tansy by GPS, wherever she went.

No more.

As I've said before, Curt in enforcer mode is scary. I had to tone him down so he didn't blast my poor little niece out of her seat at the police station.

"Tell me everything that happened at O'Berger's—again. Don't leave out any details like you did before."

Tansy's eyes welled up.

"Curt! Don't scare her or criticize her. She's just a kid. She doesn't understand what's important in this situation."

Curt looked at his shoes, long enough to threaten his image of impeccable cool. He finally sat down at the table with her, where I'm sure he seemed much less threatening at eye level instead of hovering over Tansy like a looming giant.

"Sorry I barked. We need to know what happened in vivid detail. Did anyone touch your cell?"

"Ummm … yeah, as a matter of fact." Tansy furrowed her brow and cocked her head, eyes rolled up to scan her memory.

"Just as I was getting into line to order my food, a young girl, maybe in her twenties, rushed into line behind me and asked to borrow my phone."

"Was your mom in front of you?"

"She had gone to the bathroom while I was standing in line. It was long. She didn't come back till I was almost up to the cashier.

"What did the woman look like who asked for your cell?"

"Long, black, straight hair in jeans and a pink and white ski jacket. Medium height, kind of thin. She had a diaper bag on her shoulder."

"Did she stay in line to call?"

"No," Tansy said. "She told me she forgot her phone, was late to pick up her kid at the babysitter, and needed to call in. What could I say? She asked if it was OK to move to a quieter part of O'Berger's to talk, but I didn't worry that she was trying to steal my phone. She was a responsible mom, and I could see her across the restaurant from where I stood."

"Face-on or back turned?" Curt questioned.

"Back turned. Did I do something wrong?"

"No, Tansy, you had no way of knowing. She bugged your phone when she borrowed it. She's tangled up with the bad guy that's bothering Micki and IOPEA."

Tansy looked hangdog. April was next to her, put an arm around her, and smoothed her hair.

"It's OK, honey," I said. "We just had to figure out how they put a bug on you. They can't follow you anymore now that we found it and took it off."

"So, can I go home?"

"Not yet," Curt said. "We need to make a plan."

I wondered what Curt had in mind. I was out of time for more cloak and dagger—especially the dagger—and needed to get home and get ready for the Crystal Ball. From a figurative perspective as far as balls were concerned, it was crystal; I wasn't having one.

Chapter 9

With Tansy and April inside the police station, safe for the meantime, I flashed back on my arrival a few minutes earlier. I had never been to the Taraval police station before, and my first impressions were still swimming in my mind. This branch of the SFPD is located in a foggy neighborhood in the Sunset, not far from Ocean Beach. It sits in the middle of an avenue built on a hill with residences on both sides and an urban park across the street. It has an abundance of that San Francisco scarcity—parking. As we drove up the hill, I saw the station on the left and rows of cop cars lined up on the right below the park.

The Taraval police district includes San Francisco State University and the City/County Zoo. Like most places in San Francisco, the area is both residential and commercial. It's home to numerous shopping areas in addition to Stonestown Galleria. Its Romanesque brick exterior makes Taraval look more like an old school or firehouse rather than a police station.

The station felt welcoming, both inside and outside as we arrived, even on this drab, last day of December—a day that was going downhill faster than a luge team at the Winter Olympics. The fact that 24th Street, where Taraval is located, goes uphill lent a natural perspective of things looking up and a note of optimistic contrast. Ace had arranged for us to put our heads together in the station's community meeting room. After giving Tansy the third degree, Curt wanted to talk, just the three of us—Ace, Curt and me.

"Mary Beth, would you mind taking April and Tansy to the vending machines in the waiting area? We need to do some strategizing, and I think it'd be better if the girls don't hear some of these details."

I saw by the look on April's face; she was annoyed because Curt was talking about her, as if she wasn't there. "You know, Curt, I'm 32 years old, not two."

"I realize that, April, but it's Tansy I'm concerned about. Some of this discussion is not PG-13. We'll let you in on any conclusions."

April gave Curt the evil eye but didn't resist when Mary Beth took her elbow. Tansy was already half-way down the hall, having heard the words *vending machine* and knowing they contained two of her major food groups, salty and sweet snacks.

Ace Elliot was a stout man in his mid-to-late fifties, balding with a ruddy complexion and thick, graying, mousey brown hair. He had kind, bright blue eyes, even if he often talked in a gruff manner from all those years as a cop. Even though he sounded like a grumpy old man at times, I liked him and felt safe and comfortable with him.

Ace broke the ice. "So, Micki, do you have any ideas on what kind of person might be desperate to steal your alleged secret of immortality?"

I rolled my eyes. I seemed to be doing that a lot today.

"Ace, for starters, the immortal in Immortalists stands more for our spiritual selves, our soul and how it cannot be destroyed. Our personal energy lives on in some form long after we leave our bodies. A long, healthy and productive life is what we aim for, knowing life in the spirit is eternal. We aren't looking to live forever in physical form. All of nature breaks down. We can delay the inevitable, but we can't avoid it completely. I think this guy is a nut case who thinks we can—or is desperate to believe we can."

"I see," Ace said. "So, no thought that it might be a disgruntled ex-member of your organization or anything like that?"

"I can't imagine that scenario, Ace. Every card-carrying member completes an application to join IOPEA and we have members who are psychologists or other types of mental health professionals. They help us screen for higher purpose and stability. Only twice have we ever turned down an application. We're upfront about the screening. People have to agree to it to join. We want to avoid the fountain of youth seekers and the people who take longevity lightly or care about it for purely cosmetic reasons. IOPEA is made up of caring people who want to contribute to society for as long as they can."

No one else was using the community room where we sat, but cops milled in and out periodically, looking for a few minutes' break, leaving when they found it occupied. Seeing so many boys and girls in blue felt reassuring, after all I'd been through. For a police station, I really liked this place.

Curt jumped into the conversation. "The guy's name is Foy, and he speaks with this thick brogue. I've even wondered about the Irish Mob. Maybe they want the secret so they can sell it, especially if it boils down to a commodity, like a vitamin or medicine."

"The Irish Mob has always been an East Coast phenomenon in the US," Ace offered.

"Maybe they're branching out."

"Wait a minute, Curt. I hate to burst your bubble, but I think that Foy's accent is phonier than Donald Trump's hair. I always figured Foy was an acronym, you know, FOY for Fountain of Youth."

Curt did his complete face change and turned redder than a tomato. I'd rarely seen him full-out blush, and I felt terrible. I realized I'd embarrassed him by correcting him in front of a friend and fellow law enforcement professional.

"Wow," Ace said. "I'd have never put that together."

I could have kissed Ace for saving the day and helping Curt save face, especially his red face.

"OK, so check off Irish Mob," Curt said.

"How about any personal vendettas?" Ace looked me square in the eye.

"I can answer that," Curt said. "This woman has no enemies. She's loved by so many people; sometimes I have to take a number to spend time with her."

"So, maybe Foy's an agent of Curt Stern. You hire the guy to steal her secret, shut down her immortality racket, and you finally get her undivided attention."

Ace winked! It was so out of character, I laughed louder at the kidding gesture than at the absurdity of his statement. I appreciated the comic relief.

"Yup, that's it," Curt said. "Case closed."

Ace pulled out a small notebook.

"We're all intelligent. Let's think about the kinds of people that could benefit from longer life, financially and otherwise."

"Actors!" I said. "Looking young is essential for their craft—or at least for the women."

Curt scratched his head. "Plastic surgeons and some other kinds of doctors."

"What about cosmetics makers? Companies that make beauty products?" Ace offered.

"Good one!" I raked my curls. "Religious fundamentalists who think we're playing God, trying to extend our lives."

"That one gives me a gut *yes*," Ace said.

A cop with intuition!

After more back-and-forth, we realized that even with a general idea of the types of people who might be interested in the secret; it didn't really do us much good. Where could we even start with a list that big? There must be a zillion plastic surgeons, actors, and religious fanatics in the Bay Area—even a few cosmetics firms. This puzzle could not be solved in a day, much less in the few hours before the Crystal Ball.

"Look, guys. I have a big event to get ready for. Solving it in a hurry is as unlikely as discovering a real secret to immortality, especially by the time the Crystal Ball starts in now"—I looked at my watch—"just seven hours. We have to divert Foy and get him out of our hair for now, then go into deeper pursuit after the New Year."

Curt and Ace looked at each other and grinned. I knew they were making fun of my uppity attitude, as if I knew what I was talking about. I figured I slept with an FBI agent. The ex-part didn't matter. It was just like once a Catholic or once an astrologer. Once initiated, ever a member of the club. I was learning about this spook stuff by osmosis in my dreams. Maybe that's why I had that weird one this morning.

A tall, blond and handsome officer walked into the room and handed Ace a piece of paper, a report I assumed. He definitely caught my eye. Curt may be the guy I can't get over, but I still like eye candy as much as my nieces like the mouth variety.

Ace explained, "It's the trace on the fax number Foy used for the formula. It's in an industrial area in Oakland. A warehouse near the Port that stores goods for businesses before shipping. I can make some calls and get some Oakland officers to take a look and interview the owner."

Curt got up and paced. After about a minute of repetitive motion, he announced, "I've got an idea."

"Micki, I need to trade you for Mary Beth. Go find her and stay with Tansy and April while the three of us talk cop and spy.

"I beg your pardon?"

I was insulted to be left out of the conversation. Must be a family trait. I realized I was mirroring April's irritation of a few minutes ago.

"Trust me on this, Micki."

I had to trust someone.

I got up, although slowly and reluctantly. I headed out of the meeting room. I followed Ace's directions and my instincts to the waiting room where I easily spotted my nieces with their chocolate-splotched faces. Even Mary Beth had potato chip crumb dandruff.

I succumbed to the stress and stuffed some money into the shiny contraption next to where the trio was huddled.

I ripped open the biggest chocolate bar the vending machine could cough up.

Chapter 10

I let the last square of chocolate melt in my mouth slowly, savoring it, while looking at my watch again: 1:15 PM. I wondered how long Curt would take. I needed to blow this cop stand and get ready for the Ball, hopefully with the assurance that Mr. Fountain of Youth would be deterred by whatever scheme Curt, Ace, and Mary Beth were cooking up.

Right now, a chocolate fountain was the only fountain that sounded good to me. I had forgotten just how much the serotonin boost and caffeine blast did it for me. I have to avoid sweets; they're just too addictive for me, not to mention bad for my health when eaten in excess. I have to practice what I preach or risk being as tubby as Hazel and/or sickly, not a great role model for the head of a longevity organization. Still, today, I would have dived head first into a vat of chocolate. My stress level was over the top, even after yoga and flower essences earlier. This day was a nightmare the best remedies couldn't tone down completely. No wonder I'd had a literal nightmare to start the day! I was starting to think it simply foreshadowed the quality of my New Year's Eve.

I looked up to find April and Tansy stuffing their faces again—or still. I'm not sure which. Before I could make some aunty admonition, despite my own impure thoughts that were pure chocolate, my cell phone rang. The display spelled out TASHA.

"Micki, are you sitting down?"

"Now what?" I was actually afraid to ask. I think I was trembling.

"I'm at your place. When I got to the house to drop off Snot Rag—I mean Sniffles—it was unlocked. Brace yourself. Thusie is nowhere to be found. I've combed every corner, your garden, and nearby properties."

I heard an ungodly scream. It took awhile for me to realize it was emanating from my mouth.

"Don't go anywhere or do anything until I call you back!" When they heard my hysterics, several police officers and waiting friends or relatives of people being quizzed by the cops came rushing up to my side to help.

I shooed them off. "I just got some very shocking news, sorry I overreacted." I had to confab with Curt before making any kind of official report about Thusie.

I ran down the hall, yelling over my shoulder, "You girls stay put till I call or come back." I said this despite knowing I'd likely be facing a pair of horrible bellyaches and, by tomorrow, probably an acne breakout—not to mention two whining nieces, wondering how they gained five pounds apiece and got zits overnight.

I NEARLY SKIDDED into the community room, then shot myself like an arrow to the table where Curt, Ace, and Mary Beth were sitting. They looked very wrinkly above their brows, deep in discussion.

I grabbed Curt's arm and looked directly into his blue-green eyes. I could see my desperation reflected back to me.

"Our house was broken into! They've taken my Thusie!"

"What's a Thusie?" Ace asked.

"Short for Methuselah, my very old but spry cat. I adore him. He's like my child."

Mary Beth jumped up. "Micki, I'm so sorry …"

"Honey, don't worry." Curt's turn to get up—and hug me. "Remember? I put a tracking chip on his collar on Halloween. You were so concerned that he might get out on a night when creepy people do horrible things to cats."

"That's a help, Curt, but it's not a big relief. Finding out where he is doesn't stop Foy from torturing, maiming, or killing him before we can get to him—while trying to extort information from me that I don't possess. This guy seems to know everything about me, including that my cat's the love of my life."

"Thanks," Curt said.

"OK, the sonny love of my life. You're the …" I groped for a word to convey our lack of marital status. "You're the partner love, the man love …"

"Don't overdo it."

Two beats later, you could almost see the light bulb switch on above Curt's head.

"Micki, we've never checked *your* cell phone for a tracking chip."

I handed over my phone. Curt disassembled it, and there it was.

A wave of nausea left my innards flipping like a fish out of water.

"Omigod, Curt. I wonder how long he's been tracking my every move. He never called on my cell, so I felt it was my one safe mode of communication."

I felt violated.

"Have you and your cell phone ever been parted in the past month or so?" Ace asked, in a calming tone that felt fatherly.

"I might have left it on my desk at IOPEA headquarters or in various places around my own house for a few minutes at a time, but that's it."

"Micki, I think you have to consider what I've been saying. This really might be an inside job," Ace offered.

I'd told him earlier; I was 99 percent sure I'd tripped the alarm at IOPEA last night. That meant somebody else untripped it and made the break-in possible.

"Right now I just have to get my Thusie back in one piece."

Losing Thusie would be like losing my groove. He was my familiar, my magical animal spirit in a beautiful boy-cat body. I'm sure we've been together in many past lives, as well as our present one. His longevity inspired me every day to live IOPEA's mission. Thusie made it personal, not to mention, he was my kitty son. For those of us without two-legged children, our four-leggers give us many of the benefits we missed ... and I definitely missed them.

Ace offered to ask his friends at the station to run the chip on Methuselah's collar. It didn't take long to find out that Thusie was in the same warehouse where Foy received Hans Jenner's fax about the "secret" of immortality.

The Taraval cops were great. Ace enlisted Mr. Tall, Blond and Handsome—I found out his real name was Officer Don Winter—to lead us to the warehouse in a bubble top, lights flashing and sirens blaring. Even though Don was nearing the end of his shift on a rare, slow day—it's the night shift that would be wild and woolly on New Year's Eve—it was a huge courtesy. I didn't live in Taraval's district, Thusie was lifted from another station's jurisdiction, and my boy was being held in Oakland. I was becoming more and more impressed with the loyalty and generosity of spirit the brotherhood of law enforcement, past and present, showed to one another. They took care of each other like family.

Ace had a portable LED strip for the dash in his own car that he lent us for Curt's Spider. Ace rode shotgun with Don. Curt gunned it to keep up as we ripped through city traffic to the Bay Bridge.

There had been no contact from Foy. He knew my cell phone number, but he probably also knew he lost contact with me at a police station. So, no informational ransom had been demanded for the catnapping—yet.

We burst into what looked like a mom 'n' pop, low-tech warehouse and found no one in the office. We did find a box with holes in it sitting nearby. I rushed to it. Thusie was boxed in, but looked unaffected by his adventure. For the second time today, I was so relieved; I almost relieved myself. Since I had little time for such luxuries in the day's fiasco, I looked around for a restroom to keep from embarrassing myself. I zipped in and out of the scungy unisex water closet in a blink. I knew I was in Oakland, not London, but that particular euphemism fit this tiny toilet to a WC.

Meanwhile, Don and Ace yelled around the echoey warehouse till they stirred up the guy in charge, who seemed to be alone in the huge space. I stared at box after box of goods, headed for giant containers to be shipped out of the Port of Oakland. The boxes were stamped with the names of many companies—most I'd not heard of, such as Mandarin Spa, Ravishing, and Álainn. The soon-to-be cargo all seemed to involve make-up or body care. This must be the training wheels warehouse, the cheap one you use before your company makes it big. I imagined for a few moments where these shipments might be traveling. The industrial area of Oakland is ugly, but here was beauty all boxed up, ready make a break for it.

After introducing themselves as SFPD, Ace and Don asked Richard Rawlings, who gave his name as owner of the warehouse, what he was doing with my stolen cat.

"This cat belongs to one of you?"

"Yes, me." I scowled at him. I looks could kill; I'd be kicked out of office as President of the Immortalists.

"I'm glad to see you and your cat reunited, lady. I don't know how it got here. I came back from lunch a half hour ago, and here was this box, sitting outside my office. It meowed. I was getting ready to call the SPCA if no one showed up to claim it. Thought maybe one of my customers dropped it off while doing another errand nearby, planning to come see me later."

Apparently, this guy's customers had as casual an attitude toward doing business as he did.

Ace and Don motioned us to go ahead while they continued to talk to Rawlings. I'm sure they had a lot to discuss, like how it happened that Foy had used his fax number to take delivery of information from IOPEA. Later, I'd learn he claimed to be clueless about this, as well. I started calling Richard Rawlings "Dickie Duh" in my discussions with Curt. Ace and Don stayed to check the fax for fingerprints, and I'm sure, to collect a few more duhs.

I was happy for the go-ahead to get out of there. I saw no security guard. Doesn't mean they didn't have one, but the place looked easy to break into—at least to my eyes. Note to self: Don't use Dickie Duh's storage shed. How did a guy like that stay in business? Considering the crime rate in Oakland, I'm surprised he wasn't ripped off left and right. I scooped up Thusie in his to-go box. Ace hadn't asked Curt to give him back the bubble bar. With Thusie in the car, we drove top up and used the flashing LED lights to get home in a hurry. I'd finally be able to reorient myself, get ready for the Ball—and eat!

In all this commotion, I realized I hadn't eaten either breakfast or lunch—and I'd just made my blood sugar spike with sweets. I knew an energy crash was right around the corner.

Also, during the time I was nearly frozen with fear over Thusie, I'd forgotten that Curt, Ace and Mary Beth had hatched a plan for dealing with Foy.

"So, what's the plan? What did you guys come up with for keeping everyone safe tonight?"

"Ah-choo!"

Curt asked me for a tissue and dabbed his eyes.

"Give me a few minutes to recover. It's hard to sneeze, drive, and debrief all at once."

"I've never noticed you've had any trouble debriefing me before."

Chapter 11

From Day One, Curt has always known how to play me. Today was no exception. This time he did it by the crafty way he told me about the plan he and his friends had concocted for the Ball. Neither Curt nor I—nor his friends for that matter— felt reassured by disabled phone tracking chips and Foy's silence for now about the so-called formula for immortality. Foy was a loose cannon. If Foy realized before the Ball that the "secret formula" was bogus, he'd go off, or as he put it, show me his Irish. From what I'd seen of Virginia and his escalating violence, his Irish was ugly and his presumed accomplices must be Irish, too.

In the balance was the Crystal Ball itself. The event was important to me and everyone in IOPEA. I did not want to cancel, but I would, if I didn't feel we'd be safe from Foy and his associates. Now that he couldn't track Tansy, and with a contingent of Curt's cops and ex-spies available to us for protection, I figured we had her covered. I was all ears about how Curt was proposing to handle safety at the Crystal Ball.

We sped across the Bay Bridge as his plan unfolded, the familiar metallic sound of the Spider tires ringing as we crossed the long expanse. Many people don't realize that the Oakland-Bay Bridge was built six months before the more famous Golden Gate and that the Bay Bridge is one of the longest suspension bridges in the world. I've been nervous crossing between the East Bay and San Francisco on this section of freeway ever since the earthquake of '89. The double-decker bridge collapsed, and the crush was responsible for one of the 60-odd deaths caused by the Loma

Prieta quake. At least inbound to San Francisco, we were on top, but I wasn't sure I took much solace in being the potential crusher rather than the crushee. Yeah, I'd still be here—but crushed by survivor's guilt or smasher's guilt, if my car made the fatal pancake. Curt brought me back from the fear of the moment to the fear of the evening.

"I'm telling you, Micki, this plan is ingenious, if I do say so myself."

"I take it, it was your idea."

Activate face-change sequence.

"Ace's, actually, but I added to it."

I'll bet you did. Curt had such a big ego. Sometimes I wondered how it fit in his small sports car. Thusie howled at that moment, a typical cat that hates being in a moving vehicle. The motion freaks them out—throws off their delicate sense of balance. I finally started using a vet who makes house calls rather than to spend a minute in the car with Thusie shrieking. Curt seemed to turn a deaf ear and yakked on merrily. Cats crying are like infants wailing. A woman's caretaking instincts take over. I put my finger though a hole in the box. He came to it and I stroked his head, shushing him.

"Aaaa-choo!" We'd gone a number of miles before Curt's second sneeze. I kept telling him he'd get used to Thusie's dander.

"So here's the plan. A bunch of my law enforcement buddies will come to the party. They'll come dressed like an intergalactic airport security team. You know, they'll whip up as much of a Star Trek look as each one can in a hurry, toy blasters at their hips—along with real hardware people will assume are toys, too. They'll be double holstered. A crew will man a metal detector at the entrance to the Ball. It'll be as if the guests are entering an outer space station inside. Everyone will have to pass security in order to enter the ball. We'll close down any other entrances. It fits the futuristic theme."

"I like it," I said, meaning it.

"Ace says they'll install a big sign, as folks are walking in. It'll say, 'AIRPORT SECURITY: Your Flight to the Future.'"

"Curt, this really *is* ingenious."

He folded his hand, blew on his knuckles and stroked his collar—a gesture that was one step back in time before launching a plan a few light years ahead of itself.

Even though the idea sounded great to me, I had a lot of questions.

"How are you guys going to get, much less move, a metal detector into the Moonlight Ballroom, by 6:00 - 6:30 tonight? It's almost 3:00! People coming to the Ball will think the metal detector is a toy, like the blasters. But, I get it; it'll be the real thing to make sure no one is carrying. In costume, anyone there could be Foy or his friends. We can't know who's who, including the ballroom and catering staff. There are board members of IOPEA that I won't even recognize."

Curt scratched his head. His nervous habit should have been my first clue that something wasn't completely on the up and up.

"First of all, Micki, no need to know how my friends are going to get the metal detector. They have the ability to—uh—borrow one. I realize this isn't something a civilian would be likely to know off the top of her head, but they make portable units now. They can actually go up and down in five minutes flat. They're so lightweight; you can carry them assembled on a truck. "

I pondered the visual of his friends "borrowing" one of those doorframe dealies from wherever it was normally used. I saw cloak and dagger and the Keystone Cops.

"These units are made just for situations like this, an event with a large crowd that needs security and a temporary station."

Who knew?

I couldn't help but wonder how he'd conned a number of his "straight" friends into this—straight as opposed to progressive, not gay, an important distinction best made in San Francisco.

"That's amazing. Will they use those wand dealies, too?"

"Of course," Curt assured me.

"I want to hear how you talked these guys into it—and who's coming."

"Ace is in charge of that. It was an easy sell. They all like you—who doesn't—and they're curious about the stuff you do. I shouldn't probably tell you this, so your head doesn't swell, but some of them want to approach you about your psychic and astrological skills, to apply what you know to cases."

I frowned and gave him a sideways glance. That sounded a bit much to me, considering the source. In case it was true, I was speechless.

"To answer your question, Ace will be there, Mary Beth, my old Bureau buddy Joe Castellucci, and the tall blond cop from Taraval we were with earlier, Don Winter. Maybe others. Ace is recruiting as we speak. We figure we need at least four or five—maybe six. The metal detector will go fast, but hand wanding takes more time. The more hands, the faster they get into the Ball."

The thought of seeing Tall, Blond and Handsome in a Trekkie type unitard was worth the price of admission.

"In fact," Curt continued, "Ace is a real big kid at heart and he plans to hit the Joy of Toys for blasters and other supplies. He's really into it."

Will wonders never cease?

"Are you open to a few extra embellishments?" I asked.

When Curt said sure, I let my muse take over.

"Let's play it to the hilt. Have guests strip off any heavy jewelry. When they use the hand wands, we can have the security crew tell the guests we're looking for gray spots in their aura. How can they have a nice trip at this intergalactic event, if they have unrecognized negative feelings they haven't dealt with?"

Curt admitted it would make it more customized for the crowd in question and more believable as part of the gala's theme. I offered to ask someone or ones from IOPEA to serve on the team impromptu, to provide this line of babble.

"So, the person from IOPEA fluffs the guest's aura after the wanding—that involves some hand movements around their head to clean out their energy field—and then he or she throws some star dust on them and sends them into the reception. It would be so in character and on theme. They'd love it."

Curt rolled his eyes but agreed it sounded groovy.

I managed to multitask at one point on the Bay Bridge when the City came into full view. While I listened to Curt, I drank in the Pyramid Building, Coit Tower, and especially the Golden Gate Bridge and the exquisite contrast of its burnt sienna color with the blue water below it. I thought about the much closer perspective I got of this vista when I walked or jogged on the grounds of the Presidio. This beauty was the one of the major reasons to live in San Francisco, to put up with its crowded conditions, lack of parking spaces, and to take your life into your hands, living on a fault line that could grab and shake you to death at any moment. The embrace of beauty and danger required of every San Franciscan reminded me so much of my love affair with Curt. I hated to admit it; I must like to live and love dangerously.

I had hardly recovered from this reverie when we hit the streets of the City. Thusie was fomenting some more high-pitched whine as we turned off Pine Street to Webster. In moments, home base sat perched in its serene neighborhood in Pacific Depths. Its conservative light gray and white exterior was a Victorian era façade for the futuristic leanings of its owner. I had painted the front door red, the traditional good feng shui treatment for prosperity. Even though Curt had studied Chinese as part of his training when he was in military intelligence, prior to the FBI, he insisted on saying "feng shooey" instead of "fung shway." However, he was willing to revert to the correct pronunciation so he could agree with me that our house was well "fung."

I couldn't wait to get Thusie in the door. I was starting to have fast-food hallucinations with yellow arches and the Big O's in the sky intruding on my otherwise healthy organic food fantasies. I climbed the nine steps carefully with Thusie in the Box tucked under one arm and my other hand on the banister. I admired my red geraniums in the window box on the way up, below the bay window. Even though I've lived in San Francisco all my life, I still find it amazing that flowers bloom here in winter. The color of the geraniums matched the front door and made it pop—and vice versa.

By the time I got to the threshold and inserted my key—Tasha had re-locked it for whatever good that might do—I could feel my knees weaken with hunger. I put Thusie down in the foyer, turned the box on its side, opened it and let him jump out. I went straight for the refrigerator, which was open for the next five minutes, as I did an imitation of my nieces. I stuffed my face like a Slovakian plough woman.

Chapter 12

I waddled over to the kitchen dining nook, spent from eating way past full. I was going to regret this. The base of my costume for the Ball was a leotard, and every bump and bloat would show. Maybe I could switch to a black one—more slimming.

I looked up at Hazel Hot Wheels in her usual corner as I sat down. I laughed. She looked so silly dormant, like a marionette when someone drops the strings. I felt just as limp.

Not for long.

Curt came into the kitchen, walked over to me, lifted my hair and kissed me on the back of my neck. He sent quivers down my spine to my most sensitive parts, especially when he didn't stop. His lips migrated to my ears, face—mouth ...

He pulled me up with both arms and led me upstairs to the bedroom. We flopped on the handmade quilt, shoes still on, and in my case, jacket.

"I'm not sure I've got time," I said. Cosma's digital readout said 3:15.

"Of course, you do," Curt said, pulling off his sneakers, springing his toes from cross-trainer prison. "We don't have to be at the ballroom till an hour before it starts. Even in slo-mo, you can get ready for the Ball in a couple of hours. You've got at least one to spare. I'll make it worth your while."

"How can I do it with so much on my mind? So much worry?"

"Let Uncle Curt and his love machine help you melt and moan away all your worries."

I picked up my pillow and bopped him with it. It triggered memories of the pillow fights Gregg and I had as kids. Only, believe me, with Curt there wasn't an ounce of brotherly love. This was the much hotter kind.

"That was kinky," Curt said.

He counterattacked, sending his pillow, like a marshmallow torpedo, to the tantalizing target of my loins with just enough force to stimulate without stinging.

More yelling, fighting and pillow talk—growing more erotic around the edges. Soon, we were both on fire and the flames were starting to rage out of control. I wasn't sure I could do it feeling like the Pillsbury Dough Girl. Curt would soon prove me more than capable. I was grateful he didn't jab my belly to make a dimple.

He overpowered me—knelt over me, holding me down by my wrists. After I squirmed awhile and play-protested, he let go of one hand and used his free one to slowly unzip my jacket, a tease and reminder of zippers yet to come—a preview, like a French kiss.

Before I knew what hit, clothes were peeling and flying in every direction. We were doing a love dance in precise rhythm, like a perfectly executed Tango. I could barely catch my breath—especially with an imaginary rose in my mouth.

After what felt like hours of excruciating pleasure, Curt rolled over, his eyes blazing. I had never been able to give myself so completely to another man.

We locked gazes, saying nothing for a long time. I felt an uncontrollable wave of love for him. What made it impossible for anyone else to fulfill me was the combination of play, passion and fate that always brought us back together like homing pigeons. With Curt, love and lust had always been one. What a package deal.

"Do you ever miss smoking?" he asked me out of nowhere. I hadn't smoked in 25 years.

"Not really."

"Not even after sex?"

"A little."

"I miss seeing our butts lit up together."

I rolled my eyes.

"You know where the patio is, if you need that kind of butt."

I smiled.

"I think I'll take you up on that," Curt said, "But it won't be the same."

He grabbed his robe from the closet on his way downstairs and out the back door to the garden. Cosma chimed a send-off: *The time at the tone will be 4:30 PM Pacific Standard Time exactly.*

Curt's need for a nicotine fix gave me a chance to process our love-making, this crazy day, and all the days of our lives we've been—and not been—together.

Ever talkative and word fencing out of bed, here was the one place all extraneous conversations stopped. I could hear what my insides were saying to me about him. It was always a single word: YES!

I suspected he'd hear the same word, if he got quiet enough to listen. Maybe he did and was afraid to tell me. That was a fear I could understand, even if I tried hard not to participate in it.

Separately, we are both dynamite. Together when our energies fuse, fission is only a spark away. Sometimes when we're together, in or out of bed, I need a lead vest.

My friends feel it, too. Tasha once said to me, "I'm afraid all my metal jewelry is going to fly into the two of you when you're together. The magnetism is palpable. It almost knocks me over."

Loni, my subtle mother, likens us to Elizabeth Taylor and Richard Burton when they met on the set of *Cleopatra*. Nothing could tear them away from each other, including being married to other people. Thank God, we didn't have that kind of complication. We were only married to our own fears, which probably, in some ways, was worse.

The psychic and meditation teacher who mentored me used to tell me Curt and I are power transmitters, forced to stay parallel to each other much of the time. We have to keep our distance because our full-blast combined energy tends to overload our circuits. We're a hard habit to break and an intense energy load to bear.

So, we do a lavish subconscious dance. To stand the heat of our combined intensity, without crossing the line to nuclear danger, each of us has to do what's hardest for a person used to being in power—yield. Sex is the one place we seem most able to do that ebb and flow, and our energetic choreography is much more complex than who's on top.

Truth be told, I think we both liked flirting with danger in our nuclear control tower. One false throw of the switch could destroy our relationship and leave a path of pain for us both, maybe others, in the fallout. When we were kids, it was just too hot for us to handle. We'd run—the first time, I did. Later, Curt did—over and over.

The only reason we can be together at all, is that side-by-side in the nuclear tower of our heat, we're holding hands at the controls. And now we have the maturity to back off, when we have to. I wondered if we'd reached a place where we could finally be together without running away.

Even if Curt couldn't articulate it, I knew he felt the intensity of what we have together as much as I did—and I knew someday, he'd acknowledge it. Whether that happened through learning how to stay together or bowing to the part of our passion that's so overwhelming and agreeing to go our separate ways; it barely mattered. What mattered is that we danced with this power for as long as it took to fulfill itself.

CURT CAME BACK, robe flopping, reeking of cigarette smoke—but who cared? He was carrying a cup of coffee!

"Uh oh. Bribe juice."

"I know you don't usually drink it this late in the day, but I got Hazel to whip you up a cup. I figured you'd need staying power for tonight. I don't think you got any today, did you?"

"Coffee, no," I said, getting his innuendo. He knew damn well I hadn't had a minute for any kind of normal routine. He was buttering me up. He was up to something. I knew it.

"There are a few more things I want to run by you about tonight."

Here it comes. He waited till I was defenseless in the afterglow. What a con artist.

"Ace, Mary Beth and I feel that we need to draw Foy out if we're going to foil him, no pun intended."

I had to stop rolling my eyes. I was starting to wonder if you could dislocate an eyeball.

"You mean, not avoid him? Bring it on?"

"Exactly."

"Just what have you got in mind, Curt Stern?"

I was set up. I was more of a sitting duck with my own boyfriend than the bad guy.

"We think Tansy should come to the Ball so he can go after her."

"What???" I could not believe my ears. It was out of the question.

"Curt, this guy's a crazed lunatic. You want to expose my niece and everyone at the Crystal Ball to this cuckoo? Just what we've been trying to avoid all day?"

I threw my pillow at him—again—then flopped back on the bed. This time the whack was hard and hostile.

Curt winced. "Calm down, Michele. There will be a whole contingent of former police and FBI agents there. Joe Castellucci is a trained sniper."

Curt explained that the ballroom had two small balconies like boxes at the opera. The Moonlight has a stage and theater-sized screen. The venue has multiple uses, including movie screenings. I had never even noticed the balconies when we checked out the room. Of course, I can't say I spent much of the ballroom tour looking up, except to be sure they had a nice disco ball on the ceiling, necessary to our decorating scheme. As we spoke, volunteers were hanging hundreds of tiny crystal globes— crystal balls that would complement the big mirrored ball, conveying the double entendre of our event's name. We were looking into our future. The campy image we conjured up was a gypsy or a psychic gazing into a crystal ball. When the disco ball spun, mirroring the lights throughout the ballroom, it would catch on all those other crystal balls. They'd look like stars twinkling in the sky.

Once an astrologer …

Back on Earth, Curt was trying to convince me how their scheme would work.

"Joe will dress as an intergalactic sentry. If anyone looks up, he'll wave. That allows him to stand guard with his rifle right out in the open. They'll have seen people dressed like him at the security checkpoint and figure he's part of the act. However, he'll be watching everything that's going on, ready to respond if necessary."

Was "retired from the law" freely translated, *lawless?* Worse, I could tell they were having too much fun with it—at the expense of my family, my organization and me.

"This is way too risky, Curt."

"Micki, trust me. It's not. These guys know crowd control and they know how to respond in a flash. It finally occurred to us that we were handling this whole situation bass-ackwards."

I drank it all in, raking my curls with one hand, sipping my leaded with the other. This felt all wrong, counterintuitive. Yet they were the people with bad-guy savvy. What did I know?

As usual, I had a thousand questions. Part of me could understand bringing the situation to a head, but not if anyone could get hurt.

"I have to admit, Foy's silence does not feel golden."

Curt's phone rang. It was the SFPD wanting some more details on the IOPEA break-in. At one point, they wanted to talk to me. I was happy to oblige. So far, no viable prints or suspects. No matching MO on any recent crimes. In other words, zilch. How did Foy get away with it?

I took some deep breaths and got back to my conversation with Curt about the Ball.

"How do we draw him out?"

"We let him know Tansy will be there, you'll be there with all your friends and family—and most of all, he needs to know that the 'secret' is phony."

I spend all day, running all around the City and the East Bay trying to prevent these things. Now he was telling me to do them—with gusto.

I was almost afraid to ask. "How do we draw him out?"

Curt got up and walked over to the nightstand. He held up my cell phone, rocking it back and forth a little with his wrist. He was smiling.

"What, I'm supposed to call him?"

Curt was smirking. I could tell he was enjoying knowing something that I didn't. Good thing he doesn't gamble. He'd be lousy at poker. I can always read his face. I wonder how that worked for him as an FBI agent. He's still alive, so he must have a secret agent face I don't know about. One he irons before leaving the house.

I looked around my beautiful bedroom with its well-planned combo of calming peach and cream décor. I liked it here. I wanted to dive under the covers and not come out till the day after New Year's. Maybe I could call in sick. Speaking of calling, it wasn't too late to call off the whole thing.

Curt was still holding my phone, laughing. I didn't get the joke.

"Remember when I discovered the tracking chip? That was right before you took off at Taraval to replace Mary Beth with the girls. I kept your phone till you got back. That's when we had our planning powwow. There was more than a tracking chip. There was also spyware. Foy's been tapping your cell phone conversations. After we decided drawing him out was the best course of action, I left the spyware in."

A wave of anger threatened to overtake me like a tsunami. For the second time today, I felt violated.

"How dare you, Curt! He's tracking my every move and invading my last semblance of privacy."

"There's not a lot to hide at this point. He knew you'd come home, eventually. That's a no brainer. He knows you're going to the Crystal Ball tonight—No Brainer Number Two. I've got ex-police and agents staking out our house and April's. You just need to call Tansy and tell her she can come to the Ball. Then you call Hans and discuss the phony chemistry."

Since Foy could hear everything, I was surprised he didn't show his hand when Tansy's tracking signal disappeared, but since he still had my movements and cell phone conversations, he'd barely lost a thing.

I needed to go into my home office and find some Emergency Remedy.

"If he has my phone tapped, doesn't he already know that the formula is bogus?"

"No, honey. You had that conversation with Hans on the landline— that's not tapped. I checked."

Some extra strength aspirin would be nice with an Emergency Remedy chaser. Topped with a nice antacid. My stomach was now churning, and it wasn't all from overstuffing my face.

"How on earth will I get April to agree to this?"

"She already has. I called her when I was out for a smoke."

I could have murdered him, and I would have, if I weren't trying so hard to prevent a murder—or maybe murders.

As much as I didn't want to listen, my intuition was screaming at me to yield. "Let go, Micki!" it hollered. Curt was in his element, and his eyes were bright with hope, promise, and the thrill of the hunt.

I knew nothing about this parallel universe we had entered today. I just knew that Curt's and my ability to work together and combine our powerful chemistry was being put to the ultimate test.

I hoped the whole thing didn't blow up in our faces.

Chapter 13

Curt had coached me on what I should say to whom while making my Foy-eavesdropped calls. Then he wiggled my cell phone again, an obnoxious tease before pushing it toward me.

Curt! He'd charmed April into going along with this dubious plan, concocted by his "fraternity," Coppa Spy. He skirted my buy-in until it was too late. No time left now to devise, much less implement, another plan. No wonder Curt-Micki sometimes feels like a love-hate relationship. Gotta love him for wanting to save the day and having the resources to do it. The hate comes from being played and left out of the loop. Hate is probably too strong a word … but still …

My day was becoming more surreal by the moment, as AM pushed PM. Cosma blinked 4:45 and would make her first chime of the evening in fifteen minutes. I took my cell from Curt and scowled at him. I walked over to my favorite piece of furniture in our bedroom and in the whole house, my cream-colored, cushy chaise longue. It's made of microfiber. I sank into it almost as deeply as I did every night into our memory foam mattress. The chaise enveloped me every time I sat there, curled up with a book for hours, reading by my designer arc floor lamp. The lamp held 200 watts of pink happy bulbs to combat the winter blahs and SAD. Seasonal Affective Disorder isn't as prevalent in San Francisco as it is in the Pacific Northwest, but I definitely felt my mood drop with the sunshine levels and adjusted for it. I love the autumn colors in the tiny stripes of the lampshade—so much, I did the rest of the room in matching swag chandelier and pendant lights. The smooth lines of modern furnishings mixed in with my antiques really do it for me — so Virgo, Cancer Rising. I like things that are practical but comfortable, which also honor the rich beauty of the past.

Now I'd be making calls that might determine my future and the future of a lot of people I loved.

I started with April and Tansy. Tansy answered.

"I'm sure you've heard you get to come tonight. Are you excited?" I was excited for her, probably not in the same way. More in an adrenaline surging scared kind of way.

"Are you kidding, Aunt Micki? Brady and I are pumped!" As long as you aren't pumping each other, I thought, just before berating myself for my gutter mind. I remembered my own precocious sexuality at her age … and told my mind we'd have to change the subject. I had enough worries.

At my request, Tansy put her mom on the phone.

"So, you're coming and you know the drill?" Curt told me he had alerted her to be careful of what she said because Foy was probably listening to our every conversation. By the same token, we could use his nosiness to convey information or lead him astray. It was important to establish when my nieces would arrive. Then, we had a choice. April and Tansy could actually come at that time with mega-protection, hoping Foy would pounce when the protection team was most ready to respond; or, we could announce the time and have them come at a different time, when Foy wasn't expecting it. Plan B would minimize their predictability as a potential targets. Curt thought B was safer.

"Yes," April continued. "Curt told me everything we need to know about the Ball. We'll be there at 8:30 — not at the very beginning, but after the first wave of people arrive. Since I wasn't planning to go, I've been going crazy trying to put together a costume at the last minute."

You could always go as a Slovakian plough woman on a feeding frenzy, I thought, but held my tongue.

"So, what did you decide?"

"I'll surprise you."

This day didn't have enough surprises?

The next surprise would be on Foy. Mary Beth was picking up the girls. They'd bonded during this strange day, and Curt figured that April and Tansy may as well keep the professional "bad-ass kicker" they already knew. That meant they'd be at the Ball early, since Mary Beth was part of the Intergalactic Security Squad, safely whisked in before any partygoer's hardware could hit the metal detectors.

Since I needed to get these calls out of the way and get ready, I said love-you and moved onto Hans.

"Hans, we haven't talked all day. I figured you'd want an update."

"I knew you'd call me when you had time and news," Hans said. Hans was a rock in our organization—so even-tempered and steady. He reminded me of my father.

"Well, here it is. There was an incident at IOPEA headquarters today after I talked to you. No time for details. I'll get you aside at the Ball tonight and fill you in. We also found out Foy had a tracking chip on Tansy's cell phone. Curt and his cop friend removed it. They feel confident Foy'll play nice, knowing the Crystal Ball will have a lot of police presence. Given that, Curt and his cop and spy friends think we can go forward as planned and not worry about my family being there. That's it in a nutshell. As you know, there will be a lot of information revealed tonight about how we achieve longevity. I'm sure he's gunning for that— uh, bad choice of words."

Before I could add the punch line, Hans asked, "Do you think Foy knows the formula is phony?"

"No, but I'm sure he'll figure it out when he hears my speech at the Ball. There won't be anything new in it that I haven't already told him. He's so pigheaded. I don't know why he won't believe the truth."

I nearly bit the insides of my mouth, resisting the temptation to throw a few more insults Foy's way, since he couldn't talk on this listen-in without blowing his cover. He didn't know I knew I was tapped, so I let myself have a little fun with it. Now I understood Curt's earlier smugness when he knew something I didn't about the Ball security plan.

According to Coach Curt, I just had to draw out Foy by confirming—and dangling—April and Tansy's presence at the party. At the same time, I placed a warning. There will be cops everywhere. Beware. Foy didn't want me to involve the cops; he said so. But I'm sure even Foy would realize that since I'm the girlfriend of an ex-FBI agent, Curt would have invited "guards" to the party. That turned out to be very literal.

I got up, pulled my costume out of my closet and laid it out on the bed. I was going to jump in the shower, then start decking myself out as an enhanced DNA molecule—one that represents how we're evolving from *homo sapiens* into *homo improvement*, right down to our genetic material.

As if on cue, another kind of cell rang. I went over to the table beside my chaise and saw LONI on the display. Good old mom.

"Hello, my sweet." Ugh. She was in one of those moods, dripping enough high fructose corn syrup to raise my blood sugar to diabetic levels.

"Hi, Loni. What's up? I'm busy getting ready for the Ball. I can only take a sec."

"I just haven't talked to you in a couple of days, and I've been worried about how you're doing. So much work to get ready! I hope you're not running yourself ragged."

As if my mother had a clue about hard work. She's a princess. We all inherited tidy sums from my dad's early passing. Loni managed to make a living off stretching her money from Dad and her lady-of-leisure status into a permanent condition. This was accomplished, in large part, by manipulating others and mooching off them, including Gregg and me. She was lucky Dad left her a red cent, considering they'd been divorced 14 years when he died, since Gregg and I were four and five. I always assumed Dad included her in his will to honor Loni's status as the mother of his children. I know where I got my integrity.

The thing that rankled me about my mother was her sense of entitlement. "Better than" just doesn't work for me. Sometimes I'm sure I'm adopted, and she just forgot to tell me. OK, I admit it. I keep hoping.

"I'm fine, Loni, but it has really been a day. No time to get into it."

"Are you sure you're all right, Mishka?"

"Yes, Mom."

I can't believe I used the M-word. I had called my mother by her first name for as long as I could remember. It was easy to do, since Gregg and I pretty much raised each other. The fact that she didn't mind—in fact, preferred it—said something.

Both our births were accidents—or manipulations—maybe a little of both. Loni couldn't be bothered with the warm fuzzies of motherhood. She was too busy taking care of Number One and figuring out how she could snare and keep my father or at least his support. Any time I called her Mom proved my high stress level. I barely felt she deserved the title. Loni felt more like a cousin than my parent. As my Freudian mom-slip proved, my subconscious always held out hope she'd turn into June Cleaver—or at least more the adult, if not the nurturer.

Loni continued, "It's just that you've been on my mind a lot and I have been having a sense things are not right with you."

Either I got some of my intuitive tendencies from her, or she was fishing. I wondered why.

"What about the facility. Have you checked in with them, the caterer? All the I's dotted and T's crossed?"

Why was she asking me this stuff? Loni could barely organize her sock drawer, and she was coaching me through some last-minute mental checklist? Maybe I was paranoid after Curt's manipulations, not minutes old, but I felt she was after something.

"Loni, everything's fine. We had a little misunderstanding with the caterer early on today, but it's all fixed. You'll love the menu."

Loni's a gourmand and cherishes living in San Francisco where new restaurants open weekly and her taste buds are in hog heaven. Easy to see where April and Tansy got the gene for gluttony, only Loni's tastes are way more sophisticated than O'Berger's. Loni was the first person I heard call it O'Barf's.

Loni droned on, asking way too many personal questions, as usual.

I figured anyone who asked more than I offered, considering my open nature, is prying.

"I'm so relieved to hear that it's going well, dear. And Curt will be there with some of his police friends?"

"Yes, of course."

Soon after, I said *see you later*, hung up, looked at the phone and said, *What was that?* A tiny wave of guilt passed through my mind. I knew I was short with her.

Curt was just coming out of the shower, using my unexpected phone conversation to take advantage of the vacancy.

"Loni?" he asked.

"Loni acting very weird," I said.

"What else is new?" Curt saw through my mother in a way that unsettled her. She tried to play it cool, but her discomfort was difficult to hide. I could tell Loni wasn't rooting for it to work between Curt and me, sometimes tempered by the fact that she knew Curt made me laugh and made me happy—at least half of the time.

Before we could discuss the Weird Loni Call, my phone rang again. This time it was Tasha.

"Is everything safe there tonight, Micki?"

Fair question.

"Yeah, Tasha, best as I can tell. Curt and his friends will be all over the place but not obvious because of the costumes. I don't have time to give you more details now. I've gotta get ready. Pull me aside at the event."

If I weren't careful, I'd be spending the Crystal Ball on the sidelines, updating my closest colleagues about the Day from Hell. That could take all night!

Rather than beg off, like she normally would on hearing I was time-crunched, Tasha lingered.

"I talked to your mom earlier. She heard you found Thusie. She sounded as relieved as I was when you called me. Meanwhile, Virginia's all settled in with us. Darcy is enjoying her caretaking role. They seem to like each other. How's Snot Rag doing?"

Sniffles! In the heat of everything, I'd forgotten that she'd dropped him off. To hide my mistake, I tried to find out where she had put him without admitting I didn't know. He had to be behind a closed door, or I'd have seen him by now. Plus Curt wasn't sneezing. The newer a cat's dander is to an allergic person, the more sensitive he is. Curt was getting used to Thusie and only sneezed when they were in close proximity.

Now I just had to get her to tell me whether Snot Rag was behind Door Number One, Two, or …

"Thusie didn't find Sniffles right away. Clever how you hid him."

"Yeah, I figured you spend a lot of time in your office, and it has all the kitty accessories, like a litter box in the bathroom. It'd be one of the first places you'd go. Made sense to me. I shut the door because I was freaked over the fact there'd already been one cat snatched from your house today. Not that a closed and locked front door stopped whoever took Thusie, but why make another target visible? It made me feel better."

I was now grateful she was talkative, though the idea of Sniffles getting stolen made my heart do a somersault. As soon as I hung up, I'd have to run down and check on him. One more thing to do with time running out.

Before I could say good-bye in natural sequence, I got another incoming call and begged off early. This time it was Melissa Lemon. Missy's my secretary at IOPEA.

"Micki, just checking in before the Ball. Is everything OK? Anything I should know?"

Maybe I was reading into it. It was a question any one of my right-hand staff would ask before a major event, but there was worry in her tone. As a born worrier, I recognized it.

"Everything's fine, Missy. Why would you ask?"

Foy should talk to her. He could call her Missy without insulting her.

"Oh, I dunno. Big event, spooky feeling. Someone I know who works in our cluster of buildings at the Presidio mentioned seeing Curt's car and a squad car there today …"

She, too, was fishing.

"Oh, nothing to worry about. We were just over there handling a few things I needed to do before the Ball tonight. Curt's friend was in the neighborhood and stopped by."

It wasn't exactly a lie.

"Does this have anything to do with the weirdo phone calls? Is the Ball safe?"

I was starting to sound like a broken record.

"Just show up, Missy, as planned. I'll tell you anything you need to know at the event."

They'll be taking numbers, lined up till January 2nd, for the New Year's Eve Back Story.

I ended the call in motion as I started downstairs to my office. Sniffles was snoozing sweetly on my computer chair. I left the door open so Thusie could discover him. I was happy to see that Tasha left out plenty of kibble and water. I didn't need the additional guilt trip, beyond forgetting about Sniffles, of either starving or dehydrating him due to my current lack of focus on anything but stopping a crime spree. Nothing sends me downhill faster than the thought that I'm being a bad mom, regardless of whose cat or kid is involved. Dogs I'm not so sure about.

As I rushed back upstairs, it hit me. Why would Tasha talk to Loni? They weren't friends by any stretch, and as far as I knew, their only contacts were when they bumped into each other with me.

More curious, maybe even alarming: How did my mother know I found Thusie? How would Loni even know that Thusie had been missing? I never told her. Unless Tasha told her when they talked …

Maybe Loni called my house when Tasha was there in the middle of the catnapping crisis.

Or not. It felt like something strange was going on. I was running out of time to find out for sure before I had to be in high hostess gear. It would just have to be on hold for now.

When I got back up to our bedroom, I dug my boots out of the closet. I've barely worn them in the couple of years I've owned them. When I opened the box, they had that still-new smell.

I lifted out my beige, high slouch boots. They had a nice, chunky heel. Lifts!

Since I was so worried about the effects of my pigout, I figured I should try them on first, in case my feet had swollen and I had to scrounge for Plan B footwear at the last minute.

To my surprise, just the opposite was true. I was all but swimming in them. How could I have lost weight in my feet? I've weighed 125 ever since I could remember.

That's all I needed tonight—another omen.

On the biggest night of my career, I couldn't even fill my own shoes.

Chapter 14

I love pretty and prepared. The former probably comes from having several planets in Libra in my astrology chart, ruled by Venus, the planet of beauty. I probably got indoctrinated to "be prepared" from Brownie Scouts. That's their motto. I never "flew up" to become a full-fledged Girl Scout, but Curt likes calling me one, when he thinks I'm being too Goody Two Shoes. I always feel a little bit like I didn't earn the title. After all, he earned his badge. I barely got my Brownie Cookie Sales badge before I lost interest. Even though I was never a full-fledged Girl Scout, the motto stuck.

Beauty plus Preparation equals Ritual for me. Getting gussied up to go somewhere is more than a practical chore. It's a spiritual experience. I love the transfiguration from drab to dazzling. Not that I think I'm drab in real life; I mean when I look glamorous in comparison to Everyday Micki. I guess I've never gotten over my little girl's favorite game, dress-up. Unfortunately, Loni and I never shared the same taste in clothes, so I'm probably overcompensating by still playing dress-up as an adult. Besides, Loni's feet are huge compared to mine—size 10 to my size 7's. She's a big woman. That classic picture you see of the little girl in her mother's dress, hat, beads and oversized pumps? In Loni's shoes as a kid, I looked like I was wearing high-heeled rowboats on my feet. My ill-fitting boots today weren't quite that bad, but they still conjured up the image. I could always stuff tissue paper in the toes and just get on with it. Maybe when I bought them, it was morning, before my feet had time to spread from being on them all day.

On this special night, I'd have help on my prep. Once I got to the Ball, I'd take advantage of the talents of one of our most colorful IOPEAns. His name is Reggie, and he's a retired female impersonator. After years of transforming himself into the steamy Regina, Reggie has mastered make-up techniques that could even make a bulldog beautiful. His salon is called Let's Make Up! We borrow him for all our major events. This time, we'd reserved a back room at the Moonlight Ballroom for him to do the make-up for the board members and our families. I could dress my body at home and save face for Reggie.

While I was in my office discovering the whereabouts of Snot Rag, I grabbed my performance blend flower essences that I'd mixed up earlier. Normally, I'd just have a little stage fright to overcome. With threats of more mayhem and even murder, I needed serious help from my flower friends to keep my overactive imagination in check—and to keep my cool.

Once upstairs, I was back in my chaise, shaking my dosage bottle before squeezing a few drops under my tongue.

Curt was still in a towel, looking delicious. Now that he had time to work out, his hard body took my breath away. Even with his good parts covered, our recent love fest was still fresh in mind. What was left to the imagination was still very vivid in memory. He looked damn good for 51, even without any longevity enhancements.

Curt noticed I was sneaking a lustful peek and walked over to me on the chaise. He grabbed my foot.

"I saw that! Do it again, and I won't guarantee you'll get the Ball on time—at least not the Crystal Ball."

I didn't comment. I didn't want to encourage him.

I could smell that he'd just splashed on some English Leather. I couldn't believe he still wore his vintage cologne and aftershave, just because it reminded me of our crazy youth, when we pushed everything to the limit. God, I wanted him. It's true what they say about smells evoking memories more than any other sense. I flashed on the *Night of Doing It Seven Times*, another love fest when we were in college together in the Midwest, where we first met. It's a good thing motel walls can't talk. My reputation as a Girl Scout would be ruined.

If I dwelled on these memories for another second, I'd be in serious trouble with time. I headed for the shower. A cold shower.

I TOOK GREAT PAINS to blow-dry my hair to perfection while reading a copy of my speech. I'm good at multi-tasking. I call this being a one-woman *Ed Sullivan Show*. People old enough to remember will get the comparative visual. In a figurative way, I could ride a unicycle while spinning plates on the end of rods, one in each hand, and balancing a ball on the end of my nose. Sometimes I remind myself that people with balls on their noses are usually clowns, but only when I'm at a mental Twelve Step meeting for recovering workaholics.

Curt had gone downstairs, and I was happy to have a bit of alone time before wiggling into my tights and leotards. I missed having more time to myself. I'd never lived with anyone before except for such short terms; they were more accurately classified as affairs, rather than relationships. Truth is, I never got over Curt, and God knows I tried. Sometimes I wondered if I'd ever get over him—more to the point, if I'd have to.

I couldn't go there, not tonight. I needed to do a brief, even five-minute grounding, centering and meditation exercise. I sat on the edge of the bed in my rose beige lace bra and panties. Just as I was finishing, eyes still closed, I felt the energy change in the room.

Something furry brushed up against my foot. I didn't have to look when I heard Curt padding up the stairs, emitting loud consecutive sneezes.

"Who the hell let another cat in the house?"

I felt like Lucy Ricardo on *I Love Lucy*. I had a lot of "splainin'" to do.

Before I could open my mouth, Curt said, "Tell me on the way to the Ball. We need to get going."

Curt in drill sergeant mode.

"And before we get lost in this bash and the afterglow, I need to put in a placeholder for some special time with you on New Year's Day."

Crap. I seemed to be swearing a lot more than usual today, both in my mind and out my lips. Curt was rubbing off on me—and scaring me. What was wrong now?

He must have picked up on my deep frown and the smell of worry oozing out of my pores.

"Nothing's wrong, I just want to talk about us. The start of a new year seems like a good time to talk about where this thing with us is headed."

Of all the days in all the years of our lives, Curt wanted to have this conversation tomorrow—the conversation I always wanted to have that he resisted like a root canal without benefit of anesthesia. Even a *TV Guide* blurb of this conversation was enough to knock me off my mark for the rest of the night ... if I let it.

Truth is Curt was right. It was actually three decades past time to talk, and I had a feeling tonight would hold defining moments that'd prove whether or not we belonged together.

This was the first time we'd ever cooperated in a big way, while at the same, being true to who we are. The situation required it. No Micki rolling over to soften the edges of our differences. No Curt mocking who I am and what I do, but having fun with it instead, rather than making fun of it.

I had to buck up and act from every metaphysical principal I'd lived by for the past 25 years.

I had to trust the universe to resolve every loose end, including all of Curt's and mine.

Chapter 15

The Moonlight Ballroom is located in the swank Sea Cliff neighborhood of San Francisco on premium, Oceanside property. Sea Cliff has a few commercial properties, but it's primarily a residential area. Its multi-million dollar homes sit nestled above the shore. These mansions and their perfectly manicured lawns stretch out above China and Baker Beaches. Those lucky enough to live there enjoy breathtaking views of their gorgeous surroundings, including the Golden Gate Bridge. Sea Cliff is home to many celebrities and other wealthy people who love beauty and luxury. It's easy to argue; it's the crown jewel of Baghdad by the Bay, one of the most stunning in the Tiffany necklace of neighborhoods.

Lush neighborhood aside, there were plenty of other fabulous ballrooms in San Francisco besides the Moonlight in Sea Cliff. Even the Presidio, where we worked, had beautiful rental spaces for an event like ours. They were either a little too small, too big, or to go straight to the real issue, prohibitively expensive for a nonprofit organization on our limited budget.

So, how did we get entrée to this ritzy place for our affair? The owners of the Moonlight are members of IOPEA. They gifted us the night's rental, thousands of dollars. It was a tax writeoff for them, since IOPEA is a nonprofit—and a stroke of luck for us. If it weren't for Rachel and Abner Rand, I'm afraid the concept of our silver anniversary party would still be on the drawing board for lack of the right kind venue we could afford.

Rachel's parents were ballroom dance aficionados who bequeathed several Bay Area properties to her worth megabucks. This rare and extremely valuable commercial property in Sea Cliff came with a proviso — that it would be converted into a private ballroom and made available to people who could not otherwise afford dance lessons or ballroom facilities. That's IOPEA! It was clear that Rachel inherited her altruistic qualities, and she happened to have a husband who came from the same kind of wealthy, generous background. Even better, being in this luxurious place did wonders for the prosperity consciousness of our members. We need to think big financially in order to draw the constant funding we need to do our work in the world — political, ecological, and health-related.

For now, my personal health and well-being would be vastly improved if someone would donate a car to me with heated seats. One of my friends calls them bun warmers. The closer we got to the Pacific Ocean, the more my bones ached from the damp sea air in my scanty leotards under my winter coat. My DNA wraparound was in the trunk. It'd be a last minute put-on when we arrived. My body reminded me, at times, that some of my parts are older than the rest of me looks. At least Curt, the fresh air fiend, agreed without argument to leave the top up on the Spider. I didn't want to freeze off something important this close to one of the biggest events and moments of my life, not to mention mess up my carefully primped hair. Besides, even Curt would admit that when the sun goes down in the City in winter, it's nippy.

For contrast in temperature, I flashed back to my first view of Curt in our bedroom, a half-hour ago, in his Crystal Ball get-up. He looked hot in a character actor kind of way. He was wearing a tan trench coat and a Sherlock Holmes hat. He carried the old boy's signature, S-shaped pipe. Curt pulled a magnifying glass out of his pocket to show me the complete effect.

"This is a come as you will be party, not a *come as you are*, or *come as you have been*," I said.

"Once a spy, always a spy."

Since I'd thought the same thing myself, many times, I couldn't argue with my favorite pet phrase as it applied to his life. I was tempted to point out that Sherlock Holmes was a detective, not a G-man or a G-man who was more a spy than a federal cop, but close enough. They all poked around and played with evidence. If I busted him for this inaccuracy and his face went through the change sequence one more time today, I was afraid he'd dislocate something on it along with my over-rolled eyeballs. Then we could just ditch our costumes and come as future freaks of nature, a result of modern exaggerated facial expressions.

At first, before I saw the hat and pipe, I thought the raincoat was part of a flasher costume, the way Curt was ogling me. Granted, I looked a little risqué in my base outfit—my flesh-colored leotard, from any distance, made me look naked. Apparently, our physical workout balanced my bulges. I didn't look doughy, but I still felt a little bloated from scarfing down so much food so fast.

As usual, Ira the Inventor played a big part in my futuristic costume. I was a walking, talking science project with long, blue plastic fake eyelashes. When Reggie got done with me, I'd have make-up to match in primary colors. The colors would match the corkscrew of plastic parts wrapped around me.

My loop of life resembled a flexible ladder frame with double sides. Horizontal were three-inch segments of plastic parts. They looked like tubular pasta rungs. The alphabet that spelled life was color coded to transmit genetic information, just like the real thing: red for adenine; green, thymine; blue, guanine, and yellow for cytosine.

"You look like a scientist gone nuts in a toy factory with a doll and a pile of Duplos," Curt said, as he helped me wrap the elaborate gismo around my torso—definitely a two person job. I was grateful for Velcro and the fact that Ira somehow managed to make this exacting replica as lightweight as possible.

Maybe you're wondering why I'd go to the Crystal Ball dressed as a strand of DNA. For starters, I was pretty sure no one else would show up in the same costume. As the star and host of this show, I didn't want to be like the Oscar celebrities who face that embarrassing moment of finding another woman at the gala wearing the same designer dress. So, here's my spiel on how this outfit came to be.

Deoxyribonucleic acid (DNA) is the master molecule of our cells.

Changes in the DNA of cells in organisms produce variations in the individual characteristics of a species—differences in eye, hair, and skin color, as examples. Those unique DNA signatures are what can prove a person guilty or innocent of a crime.

That's why it's maddening that Foy and his buddies didn't leave any DNA behind today! Nowadays, every crime show teaches bad guys the importance of wearing gloves and not leaving biologicals at the scene of the crime.

As to biology in a more general way, there's no doubt about the fact that DNA morphs over time. Natural selection acts on these variations in our DNA to evoke the overall evolution of the species. I believe, as do other IOPEAns that altering our thought patterns, diet, exercise and life styles are changing us at a cellular level. There's some evidence that we're actually creating a larger volume of DNA.

Here's how it all fits with my other hat I wear, astrologer.

Humanity is in a great growth spurt. Many astrological signals point to big changes early in the Third Millennium. Soon, like the ancients, we'll go back to our roots of finding meaning in the sky and living in sync with the seasons. We'll be rocking to the rhythms of the cosmos … the same cosmos that includes Earth and everyone on it.

As the wise Hermes Trismegistus said, "As Above, so Below." The earth and sky are interrelated and integrated. When we fall away from that natural relationship, we tumble into trouble. Few people realize that astrology preceded astronomy, that many respectable people not only believe in it but consider it essential. Just one example is a quote I've memorized from Hippocrates, the Father of Medicine, "A physician without a knowledge of astrology has no right to call himself a physician … There is one common flow, one common breathing, all things are in sympathy."

Most modern astrologers aren't big on predicting the future because we believe we can harness our natural talents and tendencies, combine them with the good timing astrology offers and co-create an optimal life in harmony with All That Is. We're more concerned with helping people decipher the meaning of our collective existence and our relationship to ourselves, everyone and everything else in our world—and worlds. Ecosystems, star systems—we're all in this together. Whatever happens in one part of the web of life reverberates in another.

So, the simple answer about why I'm wearing this costume? Personal and planetary evolution is my passion. I believe in the Hopi prophecy that the one-hearted people are returning, that "we are the ones we have been waiting for." Ultimately, that change of mind and heart will bring peace and wholeness to humanity.

But wait … there's more! Geneticists have been meeting around the world to decipher the significance of major changes in our DNA. Some claim the changes are so big, the last milestone of this much import was when we evolved from pond slime to legged creatures that walked out of the water.

Everyone has a double helix of DNA. The exciting news? Other helixes are being formed. In our present double helix, there are two strands of coiled DNA in a spiral pattern. The prediction? We'll ultimately develop twelve helixes. Our DNA is expanding.

You might say we're becoming more human.

I'm coming as I will be in the future—a representative of *homo improvement*. Ira rigged up extra strands in my DNA, and made the rods in the coils blink, flash and look like they're expanding or growing through use of lights and optical illusions. The battery pack he made fits behind the part of the loop that touches my waist, so I can access it easily—to turn the light show on or off. The electronics are so Ira, and this costume is right up there with Cosma and Hazel as my favorite futuristic toys.

I dressed for the Evolution.

I'D BEEN WONDERING why Curt wanted to leave for the Ball even earlier than I wanted to. He kept insisting we needed a few extra minutes before we went into the Ball to review some last-minute details of the safety plan. I figured he and his team had made a few changes over the phone that I hadn't heard about yet.

Since his urgent agenda and full focus was to update me on "the plan," Curt didn't respond, at first, to my pleas for him to hang loose about Sniffles and the sneezing. I told him I'd be able to find a more appropriate foster home for Snot Rag after January 2ⁿᵈ, while Virginia recovered in Monterey. I knew he'd heard me, after all, when he emitted one of his maniacal, theatrical laughs.

"There will be more than one way to skin a cat in the morning."

I punched him in the upper arm, but not very hard.

You'd think by now I'd be onto him. Curt was a man of a thousand distractions and manipulations. He could have easily been a magician. He had several planets in Gemini in his astrology chart. He had the Trickster expression of the sign down pat.

Even with so much personal experience of his slippery talents, Curt still caught me totally by surprise this time. He climbed the hill to the ballroom, parked, turned to me and said with no preamble, "You have to carry a gun in your boot." He pulled the thing out of his pants. The gun, I mean.

"Curt, you know how I feel about guns. Besides, I'd be carrying a concealed weapon. That's illegal."

"Whose gonna arrest you, Michele? Ace? Mary Beth? Don Winter?"

Don Winter sounded good! Maybe he could frisk me, too. I knew I shouldn't be thinking of another man patting me down while sitting next to the love of my life. As Loni would say when I made shameless noises, "Down, girl."

"And I suppose you're carrying a gun, as well?"

I knew his undercover crew would be armed, but I hadn't thought it would be necessary for Curt to join that particular party in his main role as my escort. That's when the light dawned that he would probably need a gun even more than they did. He'd be near me, and while Foy wasn't likely to kill the person he thought had "the secret," Tansy would likely be near me often. She'd need a bodyguard so she couldn't be nabbed, and Curt was probably one of many who would be keeping her in sight, ready to respond to any trouble as needed. Then, there's the fact that Curt just can't pass up an opportunity to play the hero.

Curt smiled at me, the way you do with a small child who just doesn't get it. I was grateful he stopped short of patting me on the head. I would have had to punch him again.

"Micki, the whole purpose of tonight is to have people here who can protect you against any kind of attack. Guns are essential. Somewhere in your sweet little Girl Scout mind, I know you get that."

I was quiet for so long; I could feel Curt squirming.

"Curt, if you'll recall, I didn't do so well the time you took me to target practice so I could supposedly learn to protect myself. You know, in case you aren't around?"

That could be arranged, I thought.

Curt laughed. I knew he was reliving the time the recoil nearly knocked me on my ass, and I was lucky to hit the edge of the target during the shooting session—once. It reminded me of my talent for gutter balls in bowling and why I always have hated the sport.

"Micki, some target practice is better than none. Those were bigger, badder guns. This is a compact Beretta with minimal recoil. I've been working with your boots when you weren't looking. I know it'll fit, even with your leg in it. You're right handed, so let me come around to your side and fit you out and give you your orientation."

I was nearly knocked over by a flying epiphany.

"What did you do to my boots, Curt? Why are they so big?"

"Mary Beth swapped them out for a larger size for me after she left Taraval and we went to Oakland. She went back to the mall. It was part of the plan. I wanted to be sure the gun fit. She dropped them off at our house with my key."

A fit is what I was about ready to have. I realized in a millisecond the truth of the matter. There was no use sighing or crying. It wasn't too late to back out of this plan; it was way too late. The baby was in the birth canal. Maybe not the best analogy, but at least in that scenario, I could have screamed and no one would hold it against me. In fact, no one would even be alarmed.

Curt fussed with my boot, the gun, and showed me the way it worked.

He told me I had one in the chamber and eight rounds in the clip. He wanted me to wear a spare clip in my left boot.

"What do you call this thing?"

"A Beretta Jetfire 950. It's a self-defense pistol, .25 caliber."

As if I knew anything about what that meant, except for the self-defense part. I may as well have been Curt listening to me talk astrology.

I had to admit, in that moment, the little experience I'd had with a gun made me a smidge more confident than if I'd been a firearms virgin. But I still thought Curt was crazy, thinking I'd be better off with a gun than without one. I thought the chances of someone with more experience overpowering me and turning it on me were huge. His overconfidence made me wonder how he survived two decades in the FBI without getting himself or one of his cohorts killed. I shivered. To tell the truth, I wasn't so sure about his buddies. That was probably part of the stuff he could never tell me.

That uncertainty made it even more ironic and scary that he was placing a gun in the boot of a not so sharpshooter. I was painfully aware of the expression *shooting yourself in your own foot*.

I made sure I listened very carefully about the safety—how to keep it on till I needed it, and how to flip it off in a hurry, in case I needed to shoot something … or, I hated to admit, someone.

"You have to be careful. The small grip on the gun makes it tend to bite."

Guns could bite you?

"The slide can cut the top of your hand when you fire. I'll show you how to avoid it."

I was glad the security guard for the Ballroom premises was in our line of sight—I mean, we could see him. If he had noticed this lethal lesson, he'd probably call some real cops and put us both behind bars. At least we knew the outside of the Ballroom was covered. It was the inside we had to worry about.

"You'll only get a good shot from the distance of, say, a few car lengths.

This gun is meant to protect you when someone threatens you up-close and personal. At close range, it can be lethal. But don't let distance stop you in the heat of the moment, if you need to draw. Bullets scare from anywhere in the vicinity. They push an assailant back. And you never know when you might get lucky..."

Assailant? Curt showed me how to pull out and replace the clip.

"How do we get past the intergalactic security squad?" I asked.

"They'll just press the off button on the metal detector or do a little humorous shtick around why we're setting off the alarm. We've tossed around a few ideas."

They felt liked tossed ideas, and I hadn't even heard them.

Curt took my hand to help me out of the sun yellow two-seater. The Spider wasn't especially low-slung for a sports car, but now that I had to ambulate with firearms in my footwear, I'd take all the help I could get. I was also a little woozy from taking in all this rapid-fire information that my life—or others' lives—might depend upon. I was glad we'd have a little distance to the door so I could practice walking with hardware near my feet, so I didn't look lame—literally.

Curt popped the tiny trunk and I walked behind the car to retrieve my Spiral of Life.

I was all set to represent evolving life and human oneness—while carrying a deadly weapon.

Chapter 16

Something happened to me when Curt and I walked over the threshold of the Moonlight Ballroom. I was back! I reentered my world spontaneously after spending the day in Curt's. Our worlds were about to merge again, but this time on my turf. I visualized amazing synergy and banished all thoughts of an atomic meltdown as we joined forces in a new setting—one where the good guys win.

I felt almost lightheaded leaving so much fear at the door. My daylong anxiety, at a level so over the top, was unlike me. The anxiety was also exhausting. I'd been planning this night for more than two years. The moment had finally arrived…

… and it was hilarious. The Intergalactic Security Squad was assembled just a few feet from the front door of the ballroom. They looked like a motley crew at a car wash with ray guns. Granted, they each had a regular gun holstered on their hips next to their blasters. I hoped if it came down to it, they'd draw the right one. Everyone would think these were all toys—or that we were graced with genuine security. While the ballroom was in an exclusive neighborhood, those are the kinds of places robbers get their best loot, so guards both inside and out would make a certain sense. Either way the Ball goers perceived it, we couldn't lose.

I was hoping for a more explicit view of Tall, Blond and Handsome in a Star Trek-style, tight-fitting body suit. What I got, instead, made me laugh out loud. Joe, Mary Beth, Don and Ace were all decked out in loose-fitting jump suits. Their suits were the most non-descript shade of gold I'd ever seen. For lack of a better term, I'd call it highly faded Dijon mustard. Their togs had tie closures at the neck, no pockets, and were as body hugging as mechanics' overalls.

"Where did you get these jump suits?" I asked Ace, who was the first guard at the metal detector.

"Few years back, I picked 'em up at Susanville Prison. They were surplus. They upgraded their prisoner issue, and they had a slew of them left that hadn't been imprinted with Department of Corrections yet. They made 'em available to law enforcement. Great for painting, working on your car—whatever. I still had a half dozen. One size fits most."

Don—Tall, Blond and Handsome—was the exception to "most." He looked like a fast growing boy wearing a hand-me-down suit from his much shorter brother. His uniform legs barely grazed the top of his boots.

I am very sensitive to color. While the shade of the rod squad's uniforms made me a little queasy, I was grateful Ace hadn't gotten any more recent surplus. Nearly all prisoners today wear orange jumpsuits that would cause citrus to object for the insult to its family name. I realize the loud color helps police see an escapee from miles away, but I could have seen them from the Other Side. I found the color offensive, enough to wake the dead, a three-alarm fire of pigment singeing my visual sensibilities.

The team did a great job with the Intergalactic Security sign, both the big one on a tripod as we entered and the paper version plastered on their backs. Someone had gone to the additional trouble to make a little lapel insignia—IS for Intergalactic Security—set in a background, a galaxy of stars. The paper patch was about the size of a standard nametag, and it added a touch of authenticity to the charade.

"Step right up, Ms. Micki Michaels, Queen of the Crystal Ball!"

It was Mary Beth, urging me to come through the metal detector. She beckoned, cupping her outstretched hands and pulling her fingers back toward herself. I was nervous about this *Evening at the Improv*, knowing I was carrying and about to pass through the concealed weapon equivalent of a lie detector.

After a couple of more come-ons from Mary Beth, I held my breath and stepped into the doorframe. As I anticipated, lights flashed, bells rang, and I jumped back out. It was reflex.

"Hmm," Ace said. "You need a once-over with my magic wand."

When he hovered his tool over my right boot, the thing beeped wildly, just like the metal detector.

"Oh, I get it. You're the hostess of this intergalactic gala. You're so eager to put your best foot forward, it's ticking like uranium. All that energy!"

He turned to the rest of the crew and asked, "Is she in, lady and gentlemen?"

Mary Beth, Joe and Don all gave a thumbs-up. When I walked through, bells clanking and lights blinking madly, every one applauded.

Whew! It was so real.

Curt was next. He strutted through the metal detector like a peacock. When it went ballistic, Ace raised his eyebrows in an exaggerated way and said, "Sir, I believe you're carrying. Show me your piece."

Curt gave him the two-fingered peace sign and said, "This is a love-in, right?"

Then he opened the left side of his trench coat to reveal his holster and gun.

"Of course, Mr. Holmes. All detectives must be armed to do their job. Pass!"

Once we got through our little playtime, we stood around talking with the security squad for a few minutes, before I went inside for my date with Reggie.

It was almost 7:00. None of the regular guests had arrived yet, and the only people milling around who got any glimpse of our comedy act were the caterers and ballroom staff. I made a mental note of who was watching. A girl with long, dark hair pulled back into a ponytail couldn't take her eyes off the scene. She stopped to watch, even while balancing an armload of dishes she was carrying.

Maybe Curt was right. I was getting paranoid. It was a floorshow. Why wouldn't she stop to watch? Other members of the catering and ballroom staff did. Still, something about her stood out to me. I felt I knew her, yet I also was sure I didn't.

"Where's April and Tansy?" I asked Mary Beth.

"With Reggie at the face place," she said. "He's unbelievable."

I concurred and told Curt I was going to head back to get my face done and see the girls.

"Are you coming?" I asked Curt.

"Not now. I'm going to stay and talk to the crew for a while. I'll catch you in a bit."

I told the crew that Tasha and Missy would be their aura fluffers. I'd gotten them to agree to perform this function at the Intergalactic Security point. We use a lot of glitter at IOPEA. I had a stash at home, brought it, and left it with the cops till the fluffers arrived to use it for the finishing touch of stardust on each guest's entry.

I'd have to walk the length of the empty ballroom to get to the temporary make-up salon. Good, I thought to myself. Another opportunity to try out my gun-boot walking. From Loni's gunboats, musing again on my childhood dress-up in her high heels, to gun boots tonight. I'd sure evolved.

I hate to admit it, but I think Curt's idea of swapping my boots out for a larger size was brilliant. My left foot had a bit of room left to spare in its boot, even with the bullet magazine for company, but the right was a perfect fit, wearing the Beretta. Curt must have loved the cloak and dagger of having Mary Beth and the girls head back to the mall to buy look-alikes and sneak them into my closet before we got home. I had to hand it to Curt for checking my shoe size as the baseline to expand upon, for giving her a great description of the original boots, and to Mary Beth for finding such a close match, I couldn't tell the difference—except for the odd fit. Curt was smooth. On the other hand, this attention to detail was probably a major tenet of their federal agent training.

As I found my way toward the back of the ballroom, I didn't have to search out what room Reggie was using. I just followed the laugh track.

I added to it heartily when I got my first look at April. She was wearing a warm-up suit in that ugly, prisoner orange color I just had flashed on in my mind. Sometimes psychic previews manifest in the most unusual ways.

The psychic-impression prelude wasn't funny, since it featured armed and extremely dangerous escaped cons. April, on the other hand, was hilarious. She had taken cardboard and made two long, skinny triangles, painted a shade of orange just slightly less glaring but more iridescent than her sweats underneath. She was wearing the cardboard bits like a sandwich board, attached with string over her shoulders. My junk food junkie niece was dressed, as something I didn't realize she even knew existed— a carrot. Reggie had done her face in bright green, and she was wearing a green wig with long, stringy hair that looked like the tops of carrots, freshly pulled from the ground, especially after he bunched up her leafy locks and banded them into a streaming top knot. April's lips were lined for an oversized look, filled in with lipstick in matching orange to her carrot costume. She was the funniest eyesore I'd ever seen.

"Where on earth did you get this get-up?" I asked.

"I had the orange sweats, which gave me the idea because of the color. I found a big screen TV box in the recycling bin at the apartment, so I snatched it and used the unprinted insides and some paints Tansy had on hand for her art projects."

"How 'bout the wig?"

"Tansy had it for when she played Mother Earth in the annual Earth Day event at her school."

Now she was talking and acting like a Michaels—someone with creativity whose brain could think outside the box—or in the case of materials for this particular costume, inside the box. Once in a great while, these girls actually gave me a glimmer of biological relatedness.

I had to ask her. "There's just one thing I don't get. What does a carrot have to do with how you'll be in the future?"

"Aunt Micki, you of anyone should know. You're always telling me of the importance of vegetables and how all the vitamins and minerals help keep you young. I'm a longevity snack."

Just so none of the more libidinous members of IOPEA nibbles on you, I thought to myself. I could hear Curt's frequent comment in my head, "You're such a mother hen."

April told me Tansy was in the bathroom putting on the last layer of her costume. I figured I'd get a tiny bit of R&R before I saw what she'd done to herself.

In fact, once I got into Reggie's chair, I had some of the day's precious few moments of relaxation. I even glanced at some magazines while Reggie rooted around in his various make-up cases, looking for his primary face paint. I assumed it was not something he used often, although in San Francisco, you never know. After all, SF is the home of the annual Pride Parade where the LGBT community—lesbian gay, bisexual and transgender—is known to turn out in wild attire. In the City by the Bay, outlandish costumes are what apple pie is to America. Some people dress in eccentric attire in San Francisco as a matter of course because it's the land of the free and home of the outrageous—just because they can.

I couldn't tell whether the handful of periodicals present was left behind by the rich, beauty-conscious matrons that frequented the Moonlight Ballroom or if they were take-alongs Reggie furnished. There was one called *Plastic Surgery Today*, complete with the latest procedures and ads for various kinds of treatments like Botox. I never did understand why some women were willing to pay to get a fat lip. Considering his full-page ad, it looked to me like Dr. Jonathan P. Foy was laughing his own lips, fat or skinny, all the way to the bank.

Foy! I almost sprained my neck and ripped out the page on my double take, I grabbed the magazine so hard. My heart was pounding a mile a minute.

"Down girl," I thought to myself. Surely, "my Foy" couldn't be dumb enough to use his own name. Besides, if this guy were a doctor, what MD had I ever met who would call himself Mister? I can't imagine the word slipping from his tongue in front of his surname; most doctors are so proud of the prestige of their title. He did have one of the highly suspect professions for ripping off longevity secrets... but I decided that was unlikely as Loni impersonating me to mess with the Ball's catering order. Although, note to self, assuming we got through tonight in one piece, on January 2nd, we ought to check this out along with any other Foys in the Bay Area phone listings. I suppose it's possible, even if unlikely, that "Foy" was hiding in plain sight, which is touted as the best way to do it. Still, it didn't feel right. I was still voting for FOY as an acronym for Fountain of Youth.

The cover article of a beauty industry journal caught my eye next. It was called "Beauty in Their Blood," about a cosmetics company, originally based in the UK, a family business for nearly a hundred years. The current generation and CEO was Oliver York, who now runs the company out of San Francisco. It was so sad. It showed York at the cemetery visiting the graves of his dad, Francis York, and his sister. The sister, Fiona York-Jones, died recently. Fiona's husband had died several years before her in a car accident, so she left her single brother Oliver two children to raise. I empathized because of my guardian angel auntie position with April and Tansy. His company was Álainn. Small world. Weren't there boxes from that company in Dickie Duh's warehouse? I hoped for Oliver's sake that he had better luck with Dickie's services than we did with his knowledge of the goings-on at his own warehouse.

I was a sap for any story about a close-knit family. I drew them to me like Curt's and my combined energy sucks in people's jewelry. This one really touched me. I was sorry I didn't have time to read the article to the end.

Soon, Reggie was chatting me up and patting me down with an array of powders and foundations before turning me into a crayon face. I noticed some beautiful gift bags on a side table that resembled ones he often gave out as gifts to his clients over the holidays. The holiday bags contained yummy samples of the latest make-ups, bath and body lotions.

"Ooh, what are those?" I asked.

"Swag, honey—we got swag! Just like the Oscars."

"So, what kind of promotional goodies have we got?" I giggled, hoping I was getting one of the bags. I loved the stuff.

"For you, *Mademoiselle*." Reggie picked one off the table and presented it to me with a grandiose gesture. It was made of thick brown paper with a copper raised imprint that splashed the word Earthy across the face. In smaller letters, it declared Natural Cosmetics. The handles of each bag were tied together with uncolored raffia. I couldn't wait to rip mine open.

When I dug in, I saw autumn colors of eye tint, lipstick and blush that were out of this world. They had the opposite effect on my eyes of orange prison garb. I could have dove into each little pot of prism and painted myself up like a fall tart.

"Where did you get this stuff? It's heavenly!"

"Rep from one of the cosmetics companies heard about the Crystal Ball and found out that I was working it. He stopped by while I was setting up shop this morning. His bosses thought the IOPEA crowd would love their new, natural line. Figured it might catch on with your group and get a good grounding before their launch in a couple weeks. It's not even available yet over the counter."

"Wow. I am in love! Which company puts it out?"

"It's called Álainn."

"Are you kidding? What a synchronicity. I was at a warehouse in Oakland today—long story—and saw some boxes for that company stored for shipment there. Then I read part of a story about Álainn in your magazine here just now. I thought it was French with the accent mark on the A. Said the company president was named Oliver York. I assumed the company was English when I heard his name and that the company was originally based in the UK."

"I read that story. English father, Irish mother. The company originated in Dublin but spread out to offices in London, New York, Sydney and San Francisco. The family moved to the Bay Area decades ago. That's when they moved their headquarters here."

More proof that everything is connected. My first spiritual teacher always told me that when things come in threes, the universe is getting your attention. I had encountered Álainn three times today—at the warehouse, in the article, and now in my swag bag. I wondered what it would turn out to mean.

I told Reggie how touched I was by York's story, the family legacy in the beauty business, and his losses, especially of his sister. How could I help it?

"The guy's raising a niece and nephew on his own," I said.

"I don't know him, personally," Reggie said. "His rep was new to me, too. I thought like you did, that Álainn was French. When the rep was in today, it came up in our conversation that Álainn means beautiful in Irish or Gaelic."

"Well, I'm glad for their new line. It'll be a great hit. I'll be calling Nordstrom's every two days to find out when the first shipment arrives."

I'd been so busy talking about and looking at other cosmetics, I'd barely looked at what Reggie was doing to my face. I had yellow eyelids that set off my primary blue plastic lashes, red circles in the apples of my cheeks and matching lipstick. Reggie added green to my eyebrows. I looked like a small box of basic, fat kindergarten crayons—or more accurately, like a five-year-old colored my face with them, except within the lines.

I was glad I didn't have to sit there much longer. It was too hard to take my helix on and off, so I was sitting with my hard plastic DNA loop wrapped around my torso. Pressing my back into the chair with a layer of hard plastic parts in-between was getting uncomfortable. It wouldn't be a problem for the rest of the night. I'd hardly sit down except to grab a few bites of the lavish food spread. I'd probably be grateful for some room left in my boots for my tired feet to spread.

Just as I was handing Reggie a generous cash tip I'd pre-stashed in my roomier boot, Tansy made her grand exit out of the bathroom. It was part of the suite Reggie was using, the Green Room for waiting performers when the Ballroom was in use for entertainment and dance competitions. Right on beat, Curt arrived with a tallish, fair young fellow in tow and in costume. He reminded me of Draco Malfoy in the *Harry Potter* movies, only less malefic, despite his devilish costume.

"I believe this young man belongs with you," Curt said to Tansy.

It was the first time I saw her boyfriend, Brady, and my first visual of Tansy and Brady together—in costume, no less. Tansy's get-up, in particular, made me wonder how she got it past her mom. But then, April was a lot more liberal, in general, about showing skin that I am. She sometimes calls me Auntie Grandma Moses. I don't object to the part where Grandma Moses lived to 101, but I hope the resemblance ends there.

Tansy was wearing a white, shiny one-piece hot pants outfit with a zipper from cleavage to navel. Over it, she wore a white, tight fitting, three-quarter sleeves jacket. It had Bouncer embroidered below the left lapel. She carried a soft sculpture, gold stun stick and wore a replica policeman's hat in the same satin white as her costume. Her badge on her hat read Not Yet Brigade, 2ERLY. Emanating from the middle of her hat was a gold wire holding up a golden halo. Gold, mid-thigh boots matched her heavenly headgear.

"I think I need the explanation that goes with this."

"I'm a bouncer from the Beyond! IOPEANs want to live long, and if anyone's life is threatened and they come to the Pearly Gates, I bop 'em one and send 'em back. Tell 'em it's too early."

It was so clever; I could hardly stand it. More sophisticated than I'd picture Tansy creating on her own, and way too sexy for her thirteen years, in my humble opinion.

"Hi, I'm Brady," her boyfriend said. "I'm the other half. We don't think many IOPEANs would be headed for the other place, but just in case one does something to mess up and their life is in the balance, I'm there to boot 'em out of the hot place."

Brady had on a similar get-up in devil-may-care red. His was a full-length unitard, and his boots and trim items were in black. The red hat he wore had Go Back with a thumbs-down on the badge. He also had Bouncer embroidered on his jacket. Instead of the halo through his hat, Brady had black horns popping through … and he trailed a pitchfork tail from his behind. He, too, had a nightstick, one make of polished polymer that looked authentic.

"Wow," I said. "Who thought this up?"

Brady turned redder than his costume.

"How'd you come up with it?" I was dying to know.

"My dad's a police officer. One of his old hats inspired me and his stories about bar fights and bouncers."

"Oh," Brady added. "And Tansy and her mom told me a lot about your group and the things you're into, like living a long life. I figured in the future, there should be bouncers that push people back when it's not their time to go."

I liked the way this kid thinks.

"So, Brady, since this is the first time we're meeting, I don't know the story. Tell me how you and Tansy met."

"It was at O'Berger's on Fillmore a few months ago. My mom and I live in your neighborhood, and she made her usual stop there before going to your house one Saturday."

"Tell me more about your family. Who are your parents?"

Brady "introduced" me to his mom, Teresa Winter, a social worker. Told me his parents were divorced since he was five. I could relate to that.

"My dad is SFPD. Works at Taraval station. He's here doing the door security. You know him."

Dots connecting …

"Don Winter is your dad?"

"Yeah."

Who knew? Tall, Blond and Handsome, Jr.! And senior was divorced, as in not married. Suddenly, I was very glad they got to come, though I still felt a little doubtful about their safety. If their knockout outfits weren't worth the price of admission, there was the vicarious thrill that my great-niece had a shot at the second generation of handsome Winters.

"Your dad is a very nice man."

"He told me he likes you, too."

It was my turn to blush, but you couldn't tell. After all, my cheeks that were already painted primary red.

Chapter 17

Curt came over and put his arm around me. It felt possessive, as if he could read my "impure thoughts," as one of my grammar school nuns might have called my extra-warm musings on Don Winter. For all I know, Curt could. I figure spies need a certain degree of intuition to dodge bullets and other dangers.

Maybe it was a misread or wishful thinking on my part. Curt seemed to have something else in mind.

"Come on," he said sounding urgent. He took me by the hand, led me out of Reggie's primping palace at a near trot and out into the ballroom. He kept leading me by the hand toward a dark corner. He pinned me against the wall and kissed me.

"I had no idea you'd find a science project so irresistible."

"I'm just amped up in general. I haven't had this much fun in years. All the fun of being a spy without the downside, like someone to report to and stakes higher than a kite."

"Tansy, April, me? We're not high stakes?"

When Curt got his foot out of his mouth, he said, "You know what I mean," and fished a two-way radio out of his trench coat pocket.

"What's this, Dick Tracy? Do I spy a walkie talkie?"

"Ace and the security team brought them. They think we should all be able to communicate, wherever we are in the big, busy ballroom."

It made sense to me, especially as I looked around and visualized the huge dance floor filling up. People were starting to trickle in.

"Where do I put it? I have no pockets and my shoes have a previous engagement."

"I bet we could find a few more inches in that left boot."

Curt was down on one knee, fiddling with my boot, trying to stuff in the talkie. I had a momentary fantasy of him on his knee for another reason. What a scary thought. Even if he asked me, I'm not sure what I'd say at this point.

I flashed on the fact that he wanted to have "the talk" tomorrow. I hoped he didn't have anything that drastic in mind. Actually, I was more worried in the other direction. *Not now*, I told my monkey mind.

Once I brought my brain back to the ballroom, I fully noted how spectacular it looked. The members of the decorating committee had outdone themselves. There were candles glowing on the sea of small, round side tables, covered with white linens. Each candle glinted off the free-form crystals surrounding it, forming exotic centerpieces, awaiting beautiful silverware and place settings from the buffet that would catch more of the romantic, waltzing light. I took a moment to sense more than see the ocean view at night from the floor-to-ceiling window on the main wall. The polished hardwood floors, the soft light, and the tiny crystal balls that hung from the ceiling, as well as the disco ball—everything reflected light.

I'd hope to do the same in a figurative sense this night, especially knowing there was hidden darkness in this night of pure magic.

"There you go," Curt said, finished with my boot.

Now my boots were made for talking. Curt crossed the ballroom and made a test call on the two-way. It worked just fine. I liked it. A form of protection and prevention that didn't involve bullets.

However, I did find it difficult to stuff the talkie back into my boot. It was kind of crowded in there. I decided to stick it down my cleavage instead. I was grateful for being well-endowed, because my cell phone was already occupying the place between Marilyn and Mae, Curt's pet names for "the girls." They were named after Marilyn Monroe and Mae West. No one would notice I looked a little lumpy. Or maybe they'd think that I was growing a third breast along with my other evolutionary DNA modifications. The first wrap around my body of my lattice of life covered the spot. I was grateful not just for a place to stash stuff. My costume bordered on too suggestive for its naked-at-a-distance look; I didn't need to be giving everyone a cleave shot on top of it. Not exactly a great role model for Tansy, whose evocative vestal virgin bouncer outfit screamed for help in that regard. She looked up to me as an Auntie Mame figure, the grown-up in her life who gave her an idea on how far to push the envelope. I licked mine shut at boobs hanging out.

As for my cell phone, it was on vibrate to minimize disturbance during the event. I was hoping no one called me. I didn't need the cheap thrill of my bodice pulsing at an awkward moment like the middle of my speech.

"It's getting time for me to do major meet 'n' greet," I said to Curt. "Are you up for being by my side, Gallant Protector?"

"You've got it," Curt said. He put his arm around me and walked me toward the ballroom door, the one everyone was beginning to enter. We started a reception line and other IOPEA board members joined us. Curt put an arm around me, periodically, and squeezed. He was sure affectionate tonight. Not like him to be so touchy-feely in public.

In private was another matter.

Heading the reception line at the Crystal Ball was a feast of sights and sounds I'll never forget. The *come as you will be* theme brought out more ingenuity than I'd bargained for. It looked like at least half of our guests were related to Ira the Inventor.

There were all manner of extraterrestrials. "I'm a Martian-Vulcan," one woman told me, "Because in the future there will be more intermingling of planetary races."

She looked like a green Vulcan, a short woman who somehow managed to look like the Jolly Green Giant, as though she'd dressed for success and grew into the job. Along with her green skin tone, she had antennae—dated but classic Martian images. Her firm feelers had mini-cut crystal balls stuck on the ends, tiny replicas of those hanging from the ceiling of our namesake event. They picked up the lights around the room and looked like they were transmitting intergalactic messages. Her claw-like green nails and skin, only a shade different from one another, were dusted with silver, as were her upturned Vulcanesque eyebrows and distinctive, pointed ears. Clearly, she favored her Vulcan heritage except for her skin tone and antennae. She wore long earrings—tiny chandeliers of the same mirrored balls in miniature, clustered and dancing in ever-changing colors as she picked up costumes and décor. Her one-piece leotard was splashed with a comet and trailing stars, sequined in wannabe emeralds and diamonds. They looked as authentic as jewels of the night.

Marsha Vulcan—what I christened her for my own reference—sparked an epiphany in me. In the future, we'd need to reflect our own world while bridging into advanced thought forms and new communications with an entire galaxy. Like many IOPEAns, I believe "we're not alone." Since epiphanies come to me as chain reactions, I saw how this applied on a personal level to Curt and me, as well. If I couldn't bridge between Curt, a concrete former FBI agent, and me, a metaphysical humanitarian—how would I build bigger bridges? In the future, we would all be star trekkers and creatures of at least two worlds. Until we mastered our stewardship of Earth, how could we add the stars?

Marsha Vulcan's date was a stocky cosmic cop. He looked like a burly bully with a blaster. His skin-tight silver unitard was unzipped to the middle of his he-man, hairy chest. He wore a leather necklace strung with silver bullets. His handcuffs were a bracelet on his left hand: one dangling and open, just inviting trouble to link up with him. On his back, lettering in flashing lights blinked Intergalactic Police. I was betting this guy knew Ira. I loved the synchronicity. He carried inside our surprise theme from the entryway without knowing it in advance. We had our local Intergalactic Security and Burly Blaster was part of the Intergalactic Police, patrolling the greater galaxy.

To add even more to the effect, the toes of Burly Blaster's boots were dangerously pointed, and he carried a stun stick at his belt. His hair was completely hidden under a silver hood, matching his unitard, with a plastishield window protecting his face—probably from falling meteors while he rode his interstellar space cycle. It was flipped up, I presumed so others could understand him when he talked. Along the length of his legs were flashing neon lighting bolts. He wore a high-tech version of a two-way wristwatch radio that, I'm sure, made police calls portable, anywhere in the galaxy. I wondered if there would someday be a Department of Space Vehicles in the sky. If not, what a challenge it would be to check the origins of a spaceship without benefit of license plates.

Curt nearly busted a gut laughing when he saw Burly Blaster. "What's so funny?" Burly complained, eyeing Curt's obvious detective get-up. "I'm on your side."

Burly went onto complain, "Intergalactic Security inspected my blaster at the security checkpoint just now, as if I were a common criminal."

"Yeah," Marsha Vulcan added. "That female guard said to me, 'This cosmic cop is a real hunk, honey, but you really ought to do something about your jealousy problem.' You need to send those people to diversity training so they know how to handle people of color, including green."

She humpfed and added, "Then some woo-woo woman waved a giant amethyst crystal over me to rebalance my energy, so I wouldn't look so green around the gills."

Marsha Vulcan and Burly Blaster then laughed out loud at their own charade as they moved down the line.

"It's working!" I said to Curt.

"Didn't I tell you it would?"

Curt squeezed me. His SWAT team was playing it to the hilt so well; everyone was jumping in and enjoying the fantasy.

Some Gemini came as a Walking, Talking Encyclopedia, no doubt addressing our culture's currently mounting information overload. He had a pole attached to a holder in a belt at his middle. It held menu pages of subject matter that could be flipped, like turning pages of tunes on a jukebox.

"I predict a future backlash against viewing everything on computer screens and the omniscience of the Internet," he told Curt and me, as he walked in. "Down with information monopolies."

I heard later that his talent for trivia was tapped all night, and even though he didn't carry his visual parallel to a jukebox as far as a coin slot, after awhile several people complained, "Who put a quarter in him?"

One of them was an astrologer I know, Celestial. She once suggested that all Geminis should come equipped with a built-in buzzer that goes off whenever a minute is up—a "time to stop talking" alarm. Of course, people with other signs and astrology chart patterns could use this nifty tool at times, too. I say, never mind giving the yakkety yakker an alarm. I think everyone should carry an auditory defensive weapon. It would look just like a TV remote, but you'd be able to mute the audio on people who blab on and on.

I'll have to get Ira on that …

One of the more gung-ho ecologists came as a tree, complete with a bird's nest and dropping leaves. He apparently believed that if people were going to extend human life on Earth, they'd have to become whatever the ecosystem most needs to support itself.

The "class clown" of IOPIA, Ricky Goldman, came dressed as a monkey, reminding everyone that if we reverse the aging process too far, we might find ourselves back peddling through evolution. After announcing to the receiving line that he was Longevity Gone Amok, he jumped into the arms and primary bough of the Tree Man, scratched himself under his armpits—and almost busted the tree guy's branch.

My favorite of the early arrivers was a cute, young couple I didn't recognize, probably the children of IOPEA members. They came dressed as graphic reproductions of a brain and heart. They were biology class come to life with their faces peering out like round moons from wild, soft-sculpture models of the organs. Their leotarded legs carried the replicas around the room. The girl spent all night beating her heart out, complete with ba-boom sound effects and visible beats from inside her organic costume. Every time she hugged the brain, she'd pitter-pat at an accelerated rate. He clung to her constantly, telling anyone who would listen, "The challenge of the Third Millennium will be keeping head and heart together."

He could say that again.

I could hardly get over how far everyone had gone to enact their fantasies about their future in the Third Millennium.

Curt was getting a big kick out of all this, reaffirming something I'd noticed about conservative people. Get them in a loose atmosphere and their alter egos come out. They're often as unusual at core as the "kooks" they make fun of.

The costume that made me laugh most was a guy wearing an enormous turban reminiscent of Johnny Carson's character, Carnac the Magnificent. His body was sandwiched between two boards, huge blow-ups of the standard pink While You Were Out message slip. You'd get the message whether he was coming or going. He didn't have to explain what it meant to a punster like me. I looked at him and said, "The medium is the message!" He apparently felt this would continue to hold true, probably more so, in the next several decades.

After I got his get-up, he pulled a stack of sealed envelopes out of his pocket—hermetically sealed, I'm sure, as Ed McMahon used to say. He handed them to me without a word.

"I see, we're playing Carnac."

"Hand me one," Medium Message said. His voice sounded vaguely familiar.

I followed the game plan. Medium took the envelope from me and held it to his forehead in Carnac fashion. He closed his eyes as if he were tuning into the vibes and hidden message inside.

"Micki Michaels ... " Medium finally uttered.

He ripped open the envelope and appeared to read from the index card inside.

" ... knows the secret of immortality."

"Very good," I said, trying to place his voice. I handed back the envelopes, since I couldn't linger longer. "Do I know you?"

"Tonight, all secrets will be revealed," Medium said, in a tone that sounded both playful and mysterious, as he nodded and walked away. Medium Message was wearing a red and gold eye mask that matched his turban. I couldn't figure out who he was—along with so many people present. His air of mystery really underscored the dash of excitement in hidden identities.

There was also a huge dollop of humor in nearly every costume. If there's as much truth as the experts claim to laughter as medicine, the fountain of youth is in our funny bones.

IOPEANs had humor and healing down. I was delighted how this event had brought Curt, his law enforcement friends, my organization and me into a conspiracy of laughter.

After the first fifteen minutes, I suggested we let the others handle the receiving line while I tended to other matters and touched base with various IOPEA board members. I wanted to see how they were doing on their assignments at the event.

Curt actually wanted to tag along. Every opportunity he had, he'd walk up to someone he knew—even people he didn't know. He'd grab me and say, "This is your DNA sample." Then he'd whip out his spyglass to get a closer look at me. Sometimes I was a little embarrassed by the way he'd peer down the front of me. I felt naked, even though most of my cleavage was covered by my ladder of life.

"Aha! You did it!" he'd declare to his would-be suspect. Once he called over Burly Blaster to arrest one of his pretend perps.

Sometimes he'd let them off. "Not your DNA, but where there's smoke, there's fire. Stay out of trouble."

So far, there wasn't any at the Crystal Ball. No Foy, no funny business, just a lot of good, clean fun. Could I breathe a sigh of relief—or was it too good to be true?

Chapter 18

The eye-popping costumes all around the room continued to surprise me, as I checked in with various members of the IOPEA leadership team. By now, everyone had arrived who was going to—and just in case not, members of Intergalactic Security rotated taking turns as solo guard. The other three members of the IS quartet were guarding the goings-on inside and having fun in-between. This was the key to remaining in character and going unnoticed as serious security workers packing heat. Curt and I figured the aura fluffers could have the rest of the night off after the first hour, when all but the most serious stragglers had arrived.

Now relieved of her door duty, Missy Lemon beamed in her other role as chair of the decorations committee with good reason sparkling all around us. She also sparkled dressed as her namesake, the other "Miss Lemon," secretary to Hercule Poirot, Agatha Christie's "world's greatest detective." Missy's choice honored her belief, hope and prayer—mine, too—that PBS would continue to air episodes about the little Belgian detective into the next millennium.

Missy asked me last week, "Did you know that Pauline Moran, who plays Miss Lemon on Poirot, is also an astrologer?"

"No way!"

"Way! Just like us," Missy said and smiled. I remembered thinking we need to develop a secret handshake for astrologers.

Tasha had checked in with the catering crew. I didn't grasp her costume right away.

"I'm Einstein," she said behind her moustache and gray wig. "People in the future will be much smarter than they used to be, thanks to ever advancing information technology.

Tasha gave a big thumbs-up to my question on how the catering crew was doing. I was only making conversation. I could see for myself that they were superlative in presenting and serving high-end appetizers. The small plates looked like works of art on fine china pedestals. I thought I was in the Louvre of hors d'oeuvres! There were two champagne fountains, one real and one of sparkling cider for the teetotalers and near teetotalers such as myself.

"My nerves have calmed down so much since this afternoon," I told Tasha. "If we had arrived here then, I'd be drinking two-fisted out of the one fizzing alcohol."

It was getting time for the opening ceremonies and my big speech. I wasn't nervous, which surprised me. Normally, I have pre-speech jitters. Today, I'd emptied out all my anxiety earlier like my wallet before Christmas. I had no fear left—at least for the moment.

I caught a bit of uproar near the entrance out of the corner of my eye. I should have known.

A stunning, strawberry blonde woman with huge blue eyes was wearing a midnight blue caftan with an outrageous headpiece of the globe at night, complete with orbiting stars.

"Don't look now." I said to Curt. "Her Highness has arrived."

Curt waved at Loni from the distance. I gave my mother, Her Majesty, one of those wimpy waves usually bestowed by royals on their subjects. Role reversal. Leave it to good old mom to make a more than fashionably late entrance—and to be as theatrical and outlandish as possible. It was always about her.

Loni's "hat" was out of this world, no pun intended. I figured she constructed it with the help of her friend in the cast of "the longest running musical revue in theatre history," Beach Blanket Babylon, known for its nutty headgear. Surely, it was her homage to the zany pop culture spoof and its players. I had to hand it to her. Loni came as she'll be in the future all right. She was betting we'd all still be able to see B3 for as long as we could still see. In fact, maybe IOPEA had some things to learn from this theatre phenomenon about longevity.

After acknowledging Loni's entrance, I continued my rounds. I began to notice someone missing. Ira. Where was he? I wanted to thank him for how great my costume turned out and to know his location in case of any mishaps with my ensemble. While that was more likely to happen because of radios or phones I had to fish out of my bra, I'd feel more at ease knowing his whereabouts. I didn't want my light show to short out at a crucial moment without a technician on hand.

While I was scanning another section of the ballroom for Ira, Loni swooped in. She was working her way through the crowd about the distance of three car lengths from where I was standing. She reminded me of the tutu clad, toe dancing elephant from *Fantasia*. Only her heaviest load was on her head. It was like watching someone walking around with a picnic table umbrella as her Easter bonnet.

"Pardon me," I saw more than heard her say, at least ten times in a half minute. She looked like she was trying to sit down. That would take a wide berth.

When she did, I saw Ira appear out of nowhere and head to her table. That was a sight to behold. Loni's headgear hovered over most of the full circle of the cocktail table. Ira had to sit across from her and duck under her moon and stars.

I nudged Curt. "Check this out. Loni's with Ira. I didn't know she even knew him."

"You care because …"

"I don't know, it just feels strange. Ira's the second friend of mine today that Loni has been chummy with, friends I didn't think she really knew, the other person being Tasha."

I continued to observe them, mesmerized. Curt was chatting with Medium Message, which gave me a minute to scope out the mysterious liaison between Loni and Ira.

I saw Loni stretch her hands out to Ira across the table and hold them. I could almost hear her saying, "There, there." I was vaguely familiar with the gesture, though comfort usually flowed from me to Loni in our case.

I excused myself to Curt and went to the table next to Loni and Ira, saying hello to its occupants. I didn't know them, but I figured I was the host of this bash, I could introduce myself to anyone I pleased. They were dressed as black and red peppershakers.

"The future will be a lot hotter than the present," Mrs. Pepper told me. I wasn't sure if she was referring to global warming or new advances in hard-on pills. Their peppershaker tunics were made with clear plastic front panels full of what looked like the real stuff. I wondered how they kept from sneezing in proximity to so much pepper, even if it was sealed off. They wore the shaker tops on their heads, silver caps with holes. I had mindless conversation with them within earshot of Loni and Ira, hoping to get wind of what they were saying.

I heard Ira whimpering! It was not attractive. I could not imagine what was happening. I had to find out.

"Ira! Loni! I didn't know you two knew each other."

Ira looked like a deer in the headlights. This image was even more comical, because he was wearing his Rudolph the Red Nosed Reindeer costume, left over from the entertainment at the IOPEA winter holiday party.

"We met … " Loni rolled her eyes up in that trying to remember way.

"Actually, I don't remember, Ira. Do you?"

"No."

I raked my curls. What was wrong with this picture?

"That's odd that you can't remember where you met. Ira, you seem upset. Is it because you forgot to make a costume for yourself? Why is IOPEA's high-tech wizard wearing last week's, low-tech costume?"

Ira hung his head. Was the shame that bad?

"I … I recycled it because in the future, recycling truly will be our way of life."

He took out his handkerchief and blew his nose. He looked like his mother had just died. He was talking to mine, which might kill me, but not him. He honked, and he was teary.

Soon he gripped one of my hands with both of his, looked up at me and asked in a pleading tone, "You know how very much I care about you and your family, don't you Micki?"

Was he on something?

"Of course, I know that, Ira. No question. You seem to be having a rough time over something. If you need to talk, I'm always here for you."

"I'll be OK, Micki. I almost didn't come. I have a heavy burden on my mind."

"I'm sure you can count on my mother to cheer you up."

Do not roll, I commanded my eyes. I didn't know what was wrong with Ira, but I figured he'd tell me later. It was just like him not to want to weigh me down further, when he knew I was so busy. I have to admit, though, I was concerned over his odd behavior. I'd never seen him, well, lose it. Even in his diminished state, he was there for me.

The practical part of me was relieved to know he was available physically if I needed him, if not emotionally. How ironic that he was sitting with my mother.

I had to pep things up and head toward the lectern to get the show on the road. I breezed by Curt, who was now chatting again with Marsha Vulcan and Burly Blaster.

Curt handed me a folder with my speech that he'd been keeping for me in a large, inside pocket of his trench coat.

"Hope you find a seat up close!" I kissed him on the cheek. I couldn't risk the surge of risqué I'd feel if I planted one on his lips. Talk about distracting.

The Ballroom staff had set up chairs in traditional rows for the upcoming entertainment section of the evening, including our opening ceremony, my speech, and a few more surprises. They'd take them down later for dancing.

Before I left his side, Curt touched my face, looked me in the eyes, and planted a passionate kiss on my lips.

My knees were so weak; I could barely walk to the stage.

ALL IMPORTANT EVENTS and ceremonies at IOPEA include ritual. Rituals provide a sense of continuity, constancy, and connection. Most of all, rituals encourage a sense of belonging and a core of repetitive and meaningful words and actions, a center to which we always can return. Rituals are habits permeated with larger meaning. They give our lives a touchstone and rhythm, at a community level, the same way personal rituals do—brushing your teeth, walking the dog or kissing your partner good morning.

Kissing. *Stop that*, I told myself. Curt's kiss still had me wobbly.

I climbed the steps carefully to the Ballroom stage and walked to the Plexiglas podium. The tilted surface for my notes ended at high chest level. I adjusted the attached microphone to accommodate my vertical challenge. I was grateful the podium was see-through, so I wouldn't be lost behind it, as I am with more traditional wooden ones.

Behind me was a small, live band on the back third of the platform. The percussionist struck a gong to get people's attention and quiet the room. It really worked for me, especially that clooooooossssse.

A fiery, golden, and glittery man appeared from behind the curtain to the right of the stage. Man on Fire was carrying a foot-long torch, painted gold to match. He approached the first of two floor candelabra, five feet high, on either side of the podium. He began lighting the candles, freeing the sparkle from the natural, mineral crystals placed in every other holder, between each white candlestick. There were five candles and crystals in each. After Fire Man had lit the final candle in the second candelabra, he took his place, stage right behind me.

"Ladies and gentlemen, let the opening ceremony of the Crystal Ball begin."

Cascades of waves, the ocean hitting rocks, emanated from a huge water stick and gentle chimes introduced a symphony of New Age sounds. A soft flute lured me to my center. I was in such a place of quiet so quickly, it was hard to continue my extroverted role as master of ceremonies.

"Let the sounds wash away all stresses of your day and cleanse your energy field, opening you to every possibility for fun, growth and learning on this wonderful evening of celebration—and recommitment to IOPEA's ideals and causes. Take several deep breaths and let them go. Surrender to these magical moments."

"Regulars" were used to the silence at the beginning of our IOPEA rituals, submerging themselves in the musical tones. Tonight we had many guests who were not members, so a little explanation of our customs was in order.

"Here, to set the stage for our event, are individuals representing the Four Elements—Earth, Air, Fire and Water. The four elements remind us of the basic materials of which we're all made ... and of the interrelatedness of all life. We call the energies of the Four Elements to their places in the Four Directions to help us create a sacred space for our most important ceremonies. "

Three more members of IOPEA appeared, two from stage left and one from stage right, joining our Element Fire. They posed in place until I introduced each one.

I continued, "Spirit of the East! Air! You are the Breath of Life, the Spirit of New Beginnings and Renewal. Be here now."

Air danced from the stage the moment I mentioned his name. He was a principal from the Ballet in white leotards, tights, and dance slippers with transparent strips of white, filmy material hanging from his sleeves and ankles. He leapt, followed by more graceful step-step-leaps. The current he created flapped his filmy trailers. He landed gently on his mark at the East point of the ballroom and finished with a bow.

"Fire!" I probably shouldn't have said it like that. I looked around to be sure no one was heading for the exits.

"Spirit of the South! Fire! You are our Life Force, the Sun Within. Our Vitality. Be here now."

Fire came blazing forward. He descended the stage steps and took his place in the southern portion of the Moonlight Ballroom. He was wearing a red wig with gold glitter pulled upward in what looked like an unnatural cowlick to a peak that made his whole head look like a flame. His matching unitard came alive in the subdued light, exploding red and gold sequins. Reggie had outdone himself on Fire's flaming face, gold claws, and red body paint wherever flesh showed.

"Spirit of the West! Water! You are our Emotional Intelligence, the Element that gives us depth and feeling. Be here now."

At the first mention of her name, Water sprang to life and flowed from the stage to her place in the West near the floor-to-ceiling windows with their ocean view, stroking her arms through the air, as if swimming in the sea itself. Her wild wig looked like a tangle of seaweed. Her shimmery, blue-green narrow skirt, split at the bottom, was painted to resemble fins. After a final breaststroke, she bowed.

"Spirit of the North! You are the Power of Earth—the giver of our every physical gift. Be here now."

Earth danced to her position in the North, below me. She wore a dark brown leotard and tights with cuffs of live sod at her wrists and ankles. A necklace and crown of leaves completed her *au naturel*. Once she arrived on her mark, she struck the yoga posture, Mountain Pose—fixed, stable grounded. The pose yoga practitioners normally use to start any of the standing poses, Mountain pose or *tadasana* involves becoming very still, almost as if you are growing deeply rooted out of the ground, hands at your sides, palms up. Earth moved out of her pose and bowed as I said, "The circle is formed. The Crystal Ball has begun!"

Chapter 19

When the applause dwindled—immortalists don't say *died down*—I was about to move onto our opening invocation.

But before I did, several disjointed intuitive impressions of earlier encounters jumped to consciousness. They were waving their hands to get my attention.

First was Burly Blaster. Was it really just a coincidence that he came dressed on theme with our unannounced Intergalactic Security squad? His get-up was logical as a futuristic outfit, if he had law enforcement leanings, but it got me thinking that maybe Curt and his friends might have been bugged, too, and Burly stole their idea.

Nah. Burly's get-up was complicated and Ace and Company only decided on their idea hours before the Ball. Burly couldn't have put it together that fast, even with the help of an Ira the Inventor.

Second was Jonathan Foy, the plastic surgeon with the full-page magazine ad for facial reconstruction junkies. After two beats, I pushed it down again by my previous logic. How could anyone be that reckless—to give his real name when threatening someone? Even Dickie Duh had more of a clue.

Last but not least paranoid, I flashed on Medium Message. He said I had the "secret" of immortality. Of all the things Carnac could have psyched out of his envelope, why that particular phrase? The one that had haunted me all day with an Irish accent? Medium didn't show a trace of brogue, but then, I thought Foy was faking his accent, anyway.

The word *secret* is what got me. The phrase was certainly on point with Medium's act as Carnac reincarnated, and "secret of immortality," I suppose, is a common expression, especially in the current, playful setting where, as IOPEANs, we were all mocking ourselves—a little to a lot.

Something wasn't right in the back of my mind, in addition to all that wasn't right, right in front of it. I guess with Foy's threats on hold for now, the background mind chatter became more audible.

Buzz off, I ordered my brain and its shenanigans. God, I was starting to sound like Foy in my mind. Help!

I took a deep breath to regain my composure as Micki, spiritual and altruistic leader, then continued the opening ceremonies.

"The calendar year is a new beginning, and tonight, we enter into another new beginning—a new quarter century of the Immortalists on Planet Earth Association."

The Encyclopedic Gemini stood up and shouted, "Put another quarter in!"

Applause and catcalls followed.

"In keeping with our theme of new beginnings, I have a special treat for you tonight. The IOPEA Life's the Gospel Choir will offer our invocation in song."

Behind me, emerging from both wings of the stage, came a dozen singers, decked out in IOPEA's version of choir robes. There were two styles alternating every other person. The first was a shiny, forest green version of the traditional choir robe. The choir members' banners, hanging around their necks like untied scarves, had a sky pattern studded with rhinestone stars. The second type of robe was the opposite—the sparkling sky pattern covered the robe and the banner was forest green with a globe appliqué at the bottom of each banner. It was the particular image seen 'round the world since the USA's early space program, the view of Earth from the Moon. It was the view that inspired Astronaut Edgar Mitchell to say, "We went to the Moon as technicians; we returned as humanitarians." It was the Oneness view, the one from which it's impossible to deny that humanity shares one home. It doesn't take much of a stretch to realize that we also share one heart. We're a family of humankind, regardless of all other differences.

The first strains of the band struck a familiar tune, the one made famous by The Carpenters in the early 1970s, "We've Only Just Begun."

Thus began a medley of some of the world's most inspirational songs including, "What a Wonderful World," "It's My Life," "The Circle of Life," "I Believe I Can Fly"—and more. The invocation in song concluded by going back to the beginning and "We've Only Just Begun. The choir held the last note a long time. They weren't done when the crowd went wild and the applause was nearly deafening.

Over the din, I said into the microphone, "I hope that invokes your spirits and cheerleads you onto an amazing celebration tonight."

IOPEA's Life's the Gospel Choir had roused the crowd to a revival meeting pitch. It was up to me to do something with the "school spirit."

The rubber was about to hit the road for intrigue, too. Curt and I had talked to the security team about our sense that Foy would most likely strike toward the end of my speech or just after it—that is, if he or any of his minions managed to sneak in somehow. It would sure be nice to know whether we actually had something or someone to fear. The invisible monster What-If took more energy than the Bogeyman for Certain.

Our collective logic: Foy knew the speech segment of the event was where any "secrets" might be revealed about our longevity "tricks." When they weren't, he'd be pissed, even though I told him repeatedly about what I'd shared already—that's all there is.

Foy had certainly made clear; he didn't believe what I told him was "it"—end of story. No lotions, no potions. You've got to take care of yourself, love yourself and others, and work at it.

Why did everyone want a magic pill to fix everything? Has work become just another four-letter word?

Good-bye, sweet reverie and two second mental break. It was time to scan the scene to be sure everything was set up as planned. I looked around the room for signs that everyone was at his or her station. I saw Joe

Castelluci in the bird's nest or opera box. He had his guard rifle resting, butt on the floor, holding the barrel. In the first row of seats, Mary Beth was stationed on the aisle beside Tansy. Brady was next to her, then April, with Curt covering the other "wing." Ace sat in Row 2 behind Mary Beth. Don was next to him with Tasha and Missy. I explained to Tasha who Don really was and that we were providing a little extra protection "just in case" because of the weird phone calls. Missy didn't know the details—I had no chance to bring her up to speed—and I suggested that Tasha keep it to herself for now and be sure to sit with Missy, so we could keep an eye on everyone in one cluster. They were friends. Tasha and Missy would have probably sat together, anyway.

A larger security crew would have been nice, but Coppa Spy just couldn't stir up more reinforcements on such short notice. I was happy to have the people I cared about most guarded, Foy's most likely targets— my family and co-workers who were key to the IOPEA organization.

Putting myself in Foy's shoes for a moment (would the hardware fit?), Tasha as second in command would be the next logical target to coerce or kidnap from IOPEA besides me. Unless Foy planned to beat or torture it out of me, I was probably not the target but rather the ransom provider—in information. Missy would be a potential target as someone who handled most of my communications. In his mind, she might know or have stumbled upon the "secret" of immortality.

Joe had me covered from above, as well as everyone else. Tansy and April were already established as #1 and 2 targets on the personal front. At least Foy had the brains not to go for Curt. I'm sure Curt wouldn't have hesitated to kick Foy's ass or blow his brains out, if need be. By his simple decision not to go after Curt, I think we could eliminate the possibility that Foy was Dickie Duh. At first, I thought that was a real possibility—till Dickie opened his mouth. Foy could fake an Irish accent better than acting that "out of it."

I might have inadvertently bought myself some additional time before Foy and Friends would pounce, if present. In my addled condition when I wrote to Foy this morning, I sent him a copy of my speech. I kept telling him my speech was where most of the information about longevity would be contained. Actually, more of it would be in a movie we were showing just after my talk. I was so discombobulated; I wasn't explaining myself well. The speech blended into the movie; they were really one presentation to me. They probably wouldn't be to Foy, so I was relieved I'd figured that out in time to announce something. I had to allude to it, to make sure Foy knew there was more content coming when my talk ended.

The question that kept ringing in my mind: What will Foy do when he realizes he's not going to get what he wants?

The concern evaporated as if a cartoon thought bubble had popped and dispersed when I realized I could not wait another second to speak or risk an expression no immortalist would let fall from her lips, *dead air.*

"FOR THOSE OF YOU WHO ARE NEWCOMERS to IOPEA, here as friends or family of IOPEAns, you're probably wondering why on Earth we would want to commit to having as long a life as possible, especially given some of the upheavals nowadays in nearly every aspect of living—jobs, finances, health, politics...

If you're (excuse the expression) "old" to IOPEA, maybe it's time for me to jog your memory—to remind you on this momentous occasion why we banded together to pursue long life in the first place.

Let me tell you from my own perspective, because I have a hunch that my personal experience is a lot like yours.

One day, I woke up, and I was over 40 years old. I had just begun to understand how life works—the need to live in balance and harmony, to love neighbor and self, and to contribute my talents to making the world a better place.

I realized that according to the way it usually works, half my life was over, and I had hardly even gotten started. Does that sound fair to you?"

There were shouts, *No way!* The crowd stirred and there was a chain-reaction of mumbled protests.

"That's what *I* said. Furthermore, I realized that there was no way I could have had the *maturity* to do what I needed to do to help heal myself from the natural nicks and bruises we incur on the journey of life—or to alleviate anyone else's pain—even a moment sooner. It takes living to know life. Those wounds are what keep us stuck from expressing our full potential as human beings, no matter how long or short our trip to Earth. But they are also our training wheels.

Just like everyone on it once thought the Earth was flat, some day we'll laugh at the idea that people once accepted a paltry, 80-year life-span. But we don't just want time—we want quality time. From an Immortalist's perspective, unless that life is rich, full of excitement, love, and a body that works for you, it isn't worth making longer."

Applause and hoots from the audience.

"That's why all IOPEAns live at the pulse of life and contribute their creativity and love to their planet. This is why we apply every secret, old and new, for making our bodies regenerate themselves, repeatedly. That's a life worth living.

Immortalists are not plain vanilla people. In the Big List of the Ice Cream Flavors of Life, we're the more exotic confections. (Some of us are more exotic than others. Some of us are Licorice Bubble Gum Ripple.) We definitely don't live in the center of the bell curve.

IOPEAns have too much to do to leave Earth before we tidy it up a bit. That's why I, Micki Michaels, am 'in!' I plan to live for a long time to come, if I have anything to do with it—which I believe I do. In case you haven't noticed, this is the most exciting adventure movie showing!"

When the applause broke out this time, I took the interlude to scan the crowd for the characters who had been gnawing at the back of my mind. Burly Blaster was in the third row with his date, Marsha Vulcan. They looked cute, not sinister. It took me several beats to find Medium Message. He was sitting in the right-hand back row on the aisle seat close to the single entrance/exit we had allowed open. I didn't see his message sandwich board. He must have parked it somewhere, but his turban was easy to spot as it invaded the air space of the person in the seat next to him. The only person present with bigger headgear was Loni. She was across the center aisle from him, nearly suffocating poor Ira with her headdress. Medium and Loni looked like a ridiculous pair of slightly mismatched people with big heads—overinflated caricatures. Balloons at the Macy's Thanksgiving Day Parade came to mind. With that exaggerated and amusing image, any concern I had that they could contribute to ruining my night or life dissolved.

Oops! I reminded myself I had to get back to show time.

"Once a person learns how to heal his or her hurts—that inner work that many people would literally rather die than do—Earth is Disneyland when you're ten years old and all the parents have gone home.

There's the rub, my friends. Healing hurts ... but only for a little while, and not nearly as much as the suppression of all those emotions, which is what literally kills people, slowly and often miserably ...

... along with the mass illusion that we have to die so soon. Unfortunately, mass illusions are strong psychological stuff. But we shall overcome."

The choir, settled into the first row to the left, suddenly leapt up and burst into the song of the same name. When they were finished "overcoming," I continued.

"So let's review some of the tools and tenets of living a long life to the fullest ... with many more specifics to come in our new short promotional movie to follow. Don't leave your seats! The best is yet to come."

That's for you and yours, Foy. Hold on! It's more than you got in my fax but still not what you're looking for. But if it holds you off awhile, hallelujah.

I'd better not think that too loudly, or the choir might break out into "The Hallelujah Chorus."

"Affirmations and all positive statements are key mind retraining tools that lead to the long, quality of life we seek. They are critical to use to become all that we are, instead of the meager beings we were programmed to be by well-meaning people who didn't know any better. Long life starts from inside of you. It depends on how you think, further enhanced by how you nurture your body.

But don't be fooled by the smiley-faced metafoofoo types who try to convince you that's all you have to do. Using affirmations, without inner cleansing, is like putting on a cast without resetting a broken leg. It's putting a band-aid over a severed artery. You have to be willing to dig deep into yourself, to address unresolved psychological and spiritual issues, no matter how painful. It's the key. That's part of why IOPEA has so many therapists as members!"

Laughter.

"The best illustration of what I mean goes back to the mythology of IOPEA's informal 'patron saint,' the mythological centaur, Chiron. I bet you didn't know you'd get a free holiday to ancient Greece tonight! It's essential to know about him to understand most everything we do.

Although he was half-man and half-horse, Chiron wasn't a rabble-rouser like the other rowdy centaurs. Chiron had managed to tame his wildness, while living comfortably in his dual nature, just as we are each learning to do as a spiritual being living in a human body. Chiron taught and mentored many warriors and healers like Jason of the Argonauts' story and Asclepius, the Father of Medicine. Chiron's healing was gentle, and he was especially known for his work with herbs, though he was also a surgeon.

But he was a *wounded* healer, and he was immortal. Chiron's immortality, however, was a curse to him, because he could never heal his wound and lived in constant pain. That sucks."

Laughter, murmuring.

"As one version of the legend goes, Chiron picked up a poisoned arrow shot by Hercules, his most beloved student. Chiron dropped the arrow on his foot and poisoned himself. Chiron had taught Hercules to make this poison, himself.

There are parallels, here, with modern weapons. (This is the early Greek version of shooting yourself in your own foot.)"

I winced as I said that, shifting in my gun boots, hoping once more that we could avoid any literal manifestation of that saying tonight.

"Chiron returned to his cave in agony, but because he was immortal, he could not die. Eventually, he worked out an exchange with the gods—Chiron for Prometheus, who had already been chained to a rock for eternity by Zeus for stealing fire from the gods and giving it to the human race.

(Where are you, Fire? You got that poor Prometheus into a lot of trouble!)"

Fire stood up from the middle of the room and wiped invisible tears from his eyes, as if to say he was sorry. This was not rehearsed. One of the things I love about being an IOPEAn: Our lives are sketch comedy.

"So, Chiron relinquished his immortality to put himself out of his misery. Prometheus is set free and Chiron dies. Sometimes death is the only way out of human misery.

Now, for the good news. Ancient myths are metaphorical teaching tools. They were also written for ancient evolutionary levels.

We're still following formulas that can't possibly work for us in a modern world. It's time to rewrite the endings to those myths, to update them for our evolution in consciousness.

Now that we have access in modern times to so many healing tools—physical, emotional and spiritual—there is no reason for Chiron to give up his immortality so easily.

It's time for Chiron to *embrace* it. To live long and prosper, as they used to say on *Star Trek*, to live as long as you want and your quality of life lasts. We have the technology to make that stretch, more and better, every day.

I want to close my remarks by sharing a sky hint. At the turn of our Third Millennium, the planets Chiron and Pluto were exactly in the same place, conjunct in the sign of Sagittarius.

First, if you're not versed in astrology, I should explain that we have a planet named after Chiron of myth. Just like the centaur, the half-man and half-horse I just talked about, planetary Chiron is a composite object. Chiron in the sky was the first of a new class of objects named centaurs, after mythical Chiron. These objects are half comet and half planetoid or small planet.

What does it mean? Chiron and Pluto in exactly the same place at such a momentous turn as Y2K?

The wounded healer meets the god of birth, death, and transformation. Pluto is also the planet of depth psychology, secrets, and deep inner cleansing. Pluto acts as the crucible that burns away all that is untrue or unnecessary.

We will deepen in these coming years our ability to heal our wounds, bring to light our secrets, and cleanse our inner selves from the festering pain of the past.

Then we'll be left to do our Chironic work, the part of Chiron's story I didn't elaborate on before. His skills were teaching, holistic healing, the esoteric arts, and ecology—to name just a few of his jobs and ours. It's IOPEA's job, like it was Chiron's, to lead others on the healing path we have begun to master.

Lastly, we live in the United States of America, and we are the cutting edge. Even more so, we live on the Left Coast in San Francisco, California. There are responsibilities on the leaning edge of evolution, in case you hadn't noticed!"

Laughter, groaning.

"I won't bore those of you without stars in your eyes with more astrobabble, except to say that there's every cosmic hint of huge, evolutionary changes in these first decades of the New Millennium.

Now's the time, as the Hopi prophecies say, to be the change.

I challenge each of you to extend your life and service on our mission to help the world live up to its image, the way it can be seen from the Moon—as one ecosystem and one family of humanity."

CURT'S RIGHT, I might be getting paranoid. I checked the seats while the applause-o-meter exploded. Everyone was in the same places I saw them last, both loved ones and costumed characters whose integrity I had questioned.

However, my bodice was vibrating! What idiot would be calling me at such an inopportune moment? This had better be good.

Chapter 20

I had to find a quiet corner to take the call, whoever it was. In this situation, I couldn't afford to blow off any potential communication that might impact the night's events. The timing stank because it just got noisier in the Ballroom. Everyone was scrambling, talking loudly over the noise, and many people were laughing, waving and generally looking like they were having a great time. That part pleased me.

Over the loud speaker, a deep male voice announced, "There will be a fifteen minute break until our next segment of tonight's entertainment, the movie, *The Immortal Millennium.* Please enjoy refreshments. If you leave the building, exit by the same door you entered. It's the only entrance open tonight."

I love it when a big voice you can't see makes announcements like a discarnate God. It's so commanding. No one dares disobey.

I saw half of the rod squad, Ace and Don, hurrying back toward the entrance and no doubt the Intergalactic Security point to waylay and wand anyone who came back in from a breath of fresh air—or from less invigorating input to their lungs. Since many people who go outdoors during intermission do it to grab a smoke, Ace and Don were unlikely to have too many customers in a group of health nuts. As I headed for the wings of the stage for a quiet spot, I saw my favorite part of the front row get up. Curt corralled Mary Beth, Tansy, Brady, and April in front of him. He held up the rear. They moved as a single-celled amoeba toward the exit. Curt probably needed a smoke desperately by now, but he wasn't letting his charges out of his sight, even if it meant taking them with him. I smiled to myself.

The phone, now out of my boobs and vibrating in my hand, had rung for the fourth time when I ducked behind the curtain of stage right.

I knew I was in trouble when the caller didn't talk right away. When he did, the voice was unmistakable from the first syllable uttered.

"This is my final warning, Missy. Ye had better be givin' me some usable information in that video ye've got up next, or I'll be after takin' that girl dressed so heavenly."

Foy hung up before I could respond. I couldn't run to Curt fast enough through the bottleneck of guests out of their seats and lingering in the aisles during the intermission. I'd spend half the break getting to him. Instead, I called on my Dick Tracy Two-Way Boot Stuffed Radio. Thank God, he picked up right away. My radio boot was almost as cool as one of those actual shoe phones on the old comedy spy program, *Get Smart*. The prop I really needed just now from that show was the Cone of Silence. I had to make do with a corner that was merely roaring, not blasting from the revelry.

"Curt, he's here."

"Foy?"

"Yeah—or so he says. He must be, because he described Tansy's outfit. He just called my cell."

"That must have been a thrill. I hope the phone vibes didn't hurt the girls. Worse, that I've got vibrating competition."

"Thanks for the comic relief, dear. The girls are fine. What should we do? We don't know who he is, where he's sitting, or what's going on."

"Micki, this is good. He's tipped his hand. We know he's here. You know that's better than whipping up all this adrenaline for nothing. I'll call the others and let them know. Meanwhile, if you see anything, buzz me again. I don't think he could possibly have a weapon because of the security. I'd stay put if I were you—act like nothing's going on."

"Like that's going to happen. Wouldn't you know, I have to go bad enough that I'm starting to do the pee-pee dance. It seems to me this is about the third time today that bastard has pushed me to brink of stress incontinence. And you know what an ordeal it is for me to get out of this leotard to free up my personal parts."

"You'll need the whole break to wiggle yourself in and out of your costume. I'll meet you outside the restroom by Reggie's place in five after I grab a couple puffs. I'll help you get back into your helix so you're not late."

"Well, they can't start without me! Impractical costume planning on my part. Why didn't I follow my intuition to find a leotard with a snap crotch? Thanks, Curt. Bring everyone! I want to see up-close and personal that you're all OK."

"I'll talk to the rest of the crew as I move, and I'll give you any updates when I get there."

Once Curt arrived at the restroom door five minutes later and started to rehitch me into my get-up, I felt temporarily relieved to be surrounded by my little family plus Mary Beth, who was becoming a part of it by shared experience. It was like the camaraderie on M*A*S*H. We were in the middle of something senseless together, trying to fix the wounded—but before they got hurt. Preventative medicine. That was the point of everything IOPEA advocated.

"I told Ace and Don to make *everyone* go through the metal detector who leaves and comes back in. There aren't too many," Curt said.

"Did anyone look or act odd?"

"What could be odder than this whole affair?" Curt gave me a devilish grin.

"Is it that bad?" I started to tear up. I was having a big attack of self-doubt due to the stress. I really wanted him to have a good time, even if he was an ex-friggin'-FBI agent and came from a parallel universe.

Curt put his arm around me and Helix. "Honey, I'm pulling your leg."

"I'd be careful of that tonight," I said, thinking of the heat in my boots. "It could backfire."

"Micki, it's great. You're the hottest DNA molecule on earth, and I actually dug the story time. Chiron sounds cool."

From Curt, I couldn't get a nicer compliment.

"Curt, promise me just one thing."

"Yes?" He batted his eyelashes, something he has done since we were kids that cracks me up for its role reversal—and because it personifies his manipulative dark side.

"Promise me no matter what, you will avoid violence unless it is absolutely necessary to save a life or divert a kidnapping."

"Oh ye of little faith," Curt said. "Remember, we're modern law enforcement. We live to live down those bad rumors of police brutality. And we don't want to clean up the aftermath of something messy any more than you do."

I took him at his word.

I climbed back onto the stage for the next event in our futuristic circus. I tucked my fears away, trusting that everyone was clean of weapons, thanks to the stop 'n' frisk, and that we'd find our way through this fiasco by wits or luck—maybe a combination of both. After all, wasn't I just thinking about how IOPEAns live on improv?

Our multi-talented percussionist hit his gong to signal folks to take their seats. For a minute there, I couldn't tell if Foy was calling back on my boob phone or if the next big quake had hit. Note to self: At our next event, let's find something to get the attention of the crowd that's stronger than Cosma but weaker than the sound of a blue whale in heat—or a battle of heavy metal rock bands.

Another second of that and my eardrums would rival my eyeballs for sprains and Curt might indeed have some vibrating competition. I was actually starting to get turned on.

"Ladies and gentlemen, I am pleased to share with you on this momentous occasion of IOPEA's twenty-fifth anniversary our first educational short film, *The Immortal Millennium.* In a moment, the lights will go down. I'll be joining you in the audience to see it for the first time in total myself. Enjoy!"

I made a quick exit down the stairs before someone turned the lights off and I'd have to use my DNA light show, making a spectacle of myself, to become my own flashlight. I was planning on keeping those fireworks to myself till midnight.

I scooted next to Curt who'd saved me a seat. He was back in the front row, hugging our Carrot, April. He was higher than a kite. I got a charge out of watching his little kid excitement over all this commotion—and how he got April giggling. April could get too serious at times, but that's only because she had a lot on her shoulders. I helped her as much as I could, without crossing the line Gregg asked me to walk before he died. He wanted me to temper my help to April with making sure she learned every skill to be as independent as possible. Mary Beth was talking to Tansy and Brady with great animation. When I looked behind me for a moment, Loni waved from her back row seat next to Ira. Mom, Moon and Stars could be seen for miles by her bursting bonnet. She was like a Lid Lighthouse at this seaside venue, revolving her look-at-me spotlight in a 360-degree radius.

Family all present and accounted for.

When the lights went out and the *pièce de résistance* was finally rolling, it opened with a cartoon. The voiceover announced, "The following is a production of Colorful Life Media." The words *Colorful Life Media* "ran" in from Screen Left and formed a half-circle under the bottom band of a rainbow. After a beat, the rainbow "dripped" a drop of yellow into a pot of gold. The droplet turned into a coin by some sort of magical cartoon alchemy, and then made a loud *thunk* as it dropped into the pot with the other *gelt.*

From Screen Right, a centaur galloped in on his horse's hooves with a globe in one hand. He locked all fours into a braking stop in front of the rainbow, then threw a handful of stars onto the globe like magic dust. He looked around, is if to check it out—was anyone looking at him?—then threw another handful forward at the audience, so that the entire cartoon image was overshadowed by a screen full of falling stars.

After a few seconds of stars at full-tilt twinkle, the image faded as the song "To Life!" crescendoed and the words appeared:

"The Immortalists on Planet Earth Association present ...

   ... *The Immortal Millennium: To Life!*"

A fade shot to a bird-chirruping scene in a forest of redwood trees ... a voice over (mine), reads the famous quotation from the *Immortalist's Handbook*:

> "The Immortalists on Planet Earth Association is founded on one simple, incredible principle:
>
> Longevity is a preference, an idea whose time and technology have come, and whose implications will turn your life around forever.
>
> For if you choose to live on Earth indefinitely, you will preserve Her with your very extended life. You are your own future generation who will reap what you sow.
>
> Think about it. It is a decision of ultimate responsibility, possibility, and courage."

The scene shifted. I'm standing near a giant redwood.

"Hi. My name is Michele Nicole Michaels. Call me Micki. I'm the president of the international nonprofit organization, the Immortalists on Planet Earth Association, better known by its acronym, IOPEA.

If you're watching this program, chances are you already know some-thing about the philosophy of immortality—the belief that our spirits live forever and that we can constantly rejuvenate and live much longer than ever before in our present-model, physical bodies.

Besides my job as the president of IOPEA, I am a writer and astrologer. I wrote *The Immortalist's Handbook*, considered an underground classic on open-ended longevity. At IOPEA, we consider long life a way to make our world a better place to live ...

... in fact, immortality of spirit and longevity of body make life so much better, most of us decide to stick together, stick it out, and make sure we continue to have a planet to stick *on.*

If you want to know more about immortality as a way of life, this film is for you. We'll tell you a bit about the major ways we stay young in body, mind, and spirit. If you become an initiate to immortality—if you pledge Life!—we'll teach you in more detail all the things you'll need to know to be like these redwoods someday, enjoying the wisdom of experience while maintaining vitality and beauty for as long as possible.

But rather than emphasizing techniques to stay forever young, this presentation focuses on the value of immortality as a philosophy . . . how it can change the world, and how IOPEA is already reconfiguring society, particularly in the United States, where IOPEA began and has made the most progress over the last twenty-five years.

As it says in *The Immortalist's Handbook,* immortality is a decision. This movie is slice of what IOPEA is all about, a tool to help you decide if immortality and IOPEA are for you. Long life!"

I wished we could have watched this movie in the light. I'd be scanning the crowd for signs of anyone who looked like they might be adjusting a hidden tape recorder or taking notes. Even though I felt secure with Curt and his friends and their protection skills, worry comes to me so naturally; I have a hard time flipping the switch to Off.

Soon, I was spacing out from the movie. I nearly had it memorized, since I was the primary writer. It was one of those micro-mini-rest stops, knowing there'd be no show of hand by Foy and friends till the video was over.

Then the tension started welling. I realized that as soon as the lights went up—any time thereafter—something threatening might happen. I knew Foy would never believe that the simple basics outlined in the film were all there was to it to achieve a much longer life than "normal."

He'd do something awful, as he promised repeatedly. The Bond and Bridges Brigade, as in James and Nash, had outdone itself at the stop 'n' frisk, but this only covered whatever could be sniffed out by a metal detector. God knows what else an extortionist with a screw loose might have up his sleeve or down her bosom.

Oh, no! It never occurred to me. Maybe Foy was using a voice scrambler.

Maybe Foy was a woman, and we'd been on the lookout for the wrong gender. That was already sometimes confusing enough at this party with men dressed like women and vice-versa, not to mention some of the gender-bending attire one might see in San Francisco on a typical day.

My mind started to meander wildly through all the possibilities. Soon I was deep breathing to keep myself from getting stuck in circular, nasty thought loops that only an overly active imagination can conjure up. Even with all my years of training in positive thinking, when a potential threat involved my family, my fears easily overtook me. I'd temporarily forget everything I know about "not going there."

The problem with being psychic: I have to evaluate constantly whether I'm picking up a live possibility on the collective wavelength of someone threatening or a phantom of my overly active imagination. The same open mind that breeds receptivity to free-floating thought forms tells its owner great stories sometimes.

Dana Porter snapped me out of it. She was next up on the movie and is one of my best friends. I hadn't had a chance to say more than a passing "hi" to her tonight. Dana is a gorgeous black and Native American woman whose tall, slender, and ultra-fit appearance belies her fifty-some years. Now that the intro segment was over, the heart of my passion for IOPEA was about to be revealed at the core of the movie.

Somehow, it seemed important for me to listen up. I had this strong sensation that a recommitment—or a regrouping of some sort—would soon be necessary as far as my relationship with IOPEA was concerned.

I said to my psyche, hinting at change I wasn't sure I welcomed, "What's that all about?"

Apparently, I said it aloud. Curt asked what I was talking about.

Chapter 21

Dana appeared on the video next to talk about the fourteen paths to immortality. I shuddered, knowing this was what Foy & Company had been waiting for. It was also what Foy & Company would no doubt be disappointed in.

Wearing her medical smock and a nameplate that announced her identity and credentials as "Dana Porter, MD, FACOG," Dana appeared in the comfortable waiting lounge of her medical offices.

"I'm Dr. Dana Porter, a holistic gynecologist, and a board member of IOPEA. I am also trained as a massage therapist, herbologist, and flower essence practitioner—among other things.

If you're watching this film because you're interested in how we, at IOPEA, stay looking so young (I was 54 on my last birthday), you'll be interested in many of the things I'm about to tell you. Let's go into our classroom, where I can get a little help from our friend and mascot, the Centaur.

In a technique of combining live people with cartoons, first made popular in the late 1980s, the IOPEA cartoon centaur appeared at the board with a pointer in hand, ready to help Dana teach her lessons on immortality. These fourteen key words were listed on the board:

1. Truth
2. Company
3. Trauma (birth and life)
4. Vitamins, herbs, etc.
5. Substances (no alcohol, drugs, smoking)
6. Responsible sex
7. Vegetarian
8. Fasting
9. Bathing
10. Gravity
11. Forgive
12. Fear
13. Active
14. Imagination

As Dana touched on each topic, the centaur pointed to it on the board. The key word or words would light up when he pointed, while the other writing on the white board faded. Then each key phrase became the heading on a blank white board. Onto this "clean slate" was projected a scene, depicting the particular path to immortality Dana was addressing at the moment.

On the path of *Truth*, Dana's voiceover accompanied a birthing scene. "This is the truth." Over the projection of a cemetery, she commented, "The idea that you have to end up here at a time dictated by statistics is the lie." Dana came back from the cemetery quickly to continue talking to us from her office, which made me happy. Graveyards creep me out.

"In the Bible," Dana continued, "Methuselah lived 969 years. Granted, more recent studies conclude that we might have mistranslated this whopping big number, but even adjusting for the error, Methuselah lived exceptionally long for his day. There are five immortal masters listed in the Bible, as well: Elijah, Enoch, Jesus, Melchizedek, and Moses. The resurrection of Jesus depicts his ability, as an ascended master, to materialize and dematerialize at will. Most IOPEAns feel the Bible is metaphorical. Still, these claims get my attention, even if they're symbolic. They are startling, and they suggest there's more to life and our physical potentials than we'd ever imagined. I have personally met individuals in India, Tibet, and elsewhere, who claim to be over three hundred years old.

So, why do we settle for a flimsy 80 years? The truth is that *you don't have to*. Many of us weren't taught the skills to give us peace and joy here on Earth, so death is our escape. We learn from an early age to accept the maxim, *life is short*. We keep death in our hip pocket as our way out and create an early exit, if we feel the need. Life is painful; so, death comes eventually as a relief and a reward.

Through the immortality movement, we learn those skills for healing our emotional traumas and learning to trust life. With those skills, we don't want out—we want in!

Do some of your own research and discover that life spans have varied widely throughout human history. At this stage of our evolution, longevity is natural. Reincarnation has all but been proven in countless research projects backed by modern physics. It's a question of completing what you came to learn on Planet Earth, either now or later. Why go through birth, childhood, and adolescence—the hard part—endless times? We can shorten the number of trips till the ultimate time when we claim our true immortality as pure spirit and don't bother to come back."

Dana inspired me. I found myself mesmerized by her presentation that I had not heard for so long, it felt brand new.

"Your greatest challenge in considering immortality as a lifestyle is turning around the deadly thinking that inundates our culture. At IO-PEA, we love life! Death is just a transition to more life in another form, but you don't have to give up when you're on a roll, to cut short your current lifetime before you've seen all the sights and had all your fun to go onto the next trip on your reincarnational itinerary. We are willing to help you learn this truth—to embrace the immortality of your spirit and the longevity of your body."

On the path of *Company*, Dana talked about the importance of spending time with other people who believe in immortality of spirit and longevity of body—or at least those willing to allow an immortalist his or her beliefs without writing them off as crazy.

"Nearly the entire human race believes in the statistical average life span, those morbidity tables used by agents to calculate the cost of your life insurance policy. You are not a statistic. Someone has to be at the livelong end of the bell curve. The idea that the best you can do is only a little bit better than average? This is a tough consciousness to overcome. The good news is that the more people who join the immortality movement, the less you are alone. It's crucial to be with people who support your belief in what others think is 'impossible.'

Of course, you can't avoid most of the human race in daily living. At the very least, make your closest friends immortalists, and avoid buying into 'consensus reality' about life span. You do not have to consent to those limits or make them your reality."

Birth and life trauma began with Dana's assisting a water birth with dark lights and gentle music, designed to minimize the stress of delivery. The first scene dissolved into a breath therapy session with a client and an IOPEAn breathing coach. The client was reliving an especially difficult, earlier life event.

Dana said, "I have had the honor of assisting in more human births than I can count during the course of my medical career. Birth is not an easy process. Many therapists and holistic healers have been instrumental in teaching us about the emotional wounding experienced by the body-mind-spirit through the shock of coming into incarnation. This should be reason enough not to die and be reborn with excess repetition. Choose fewer lives and stick with one that's going well for as long as it works in the positive.

For most of us, our actual delivery is just the beginning of the pain we encounter. Emotions, not released, either during birth or other traumas, tend to get 'stuck' in our psyches, acting as blockages to creating what we want in life. During these traumas, we tend to make negative decisions about life. We encapsulate them into repetitive mottos in our brains, often unconsciously; phrases like *I'm not enough* or *Love is painful*. Until the experience can be recreated and the negative impression we've lived by is released, we are blocked emotionally—limited in what we can experience of joy and aliveness. As I'm sure you can imagine, if you have the belief, *love is pain;* your entire being creates that experience for you to sustain your conviction, to make you 'right.' We are what we think and believe.

The breath of life itself is the cure to most human suffering! All IO-PEAns are taught these techniques, learning to connect the inhale and exhale for extended periods—at first, with a coach.

The results of breath therapy are usually the spontaneous recollection and release of past emotional trauma, even back as far as our own births. We become aware of the subconscious decisions we made during those unpleasant experiences. Finally, we can change them.

For example, I was born in the 1950s, when drugs were routinely administered to mothers in labor. Many people of my generation were quite literally born 'stoned,' confused and more or less drunk on medication. We often made a subconscious decision, 'Life is confusing.' The connection between this practice and a generation of drug and alcohol abusers is obvious! When we felt insecure and wanted to go 'back to the womb,' so to speak, it meant going back to a state of intoxication.

Most of us have found this self-improvement work, catalyzed by breath therapy, is far more effective than traditional therapy alone and its best complement. This is that 'inner work' you often hear immortalists speak about—the cure that is sometimes painful in the process, but totally liberating in the completion."

Under *Vitamins, herbs, etc.*, Dana talked about many of the vitamins, herbs, essential oils, and flower essences that help foster longevity. She emphasized that none of these things in and of themselves would extend life—only a coordinated program that addressed body, mind, and spirit. The centaur's board lit up with various flowers and herbs, illustrating Dana's pharmacopoeia segment.

Dana began speaking about *No alcohol, drugs, smoking*. As the centaur pointed to the subject, a bar scene projected onto the board inside a traditional red circle with a vertical slash to indicate "forbidden." Dr. Dana commented:

"As a physician, of course I'm nix on alcohol, drugs, and smoking. As a holistic physician, I barely believe in prescribing *aspirin*, if there's a more natural alternative.

It's ironic that the substances we have traditionally abused in celebrating life are the very ones that suppress it. How can we be fully alive, operating on 'slow?' Also, if the breath is the very substance of aliveness and healing, to repress that force by inhaling a smokescreen makes little sense.

The immortalist lifestyle leads to natural highs—free as the air you breathe. We aren't extremists. Many of us still have wine, now and then. We find, however, with the purification of our systems from whole foods and other health practices; our tolerance for even a little alcohol becomes minimal. Few of us miss it and substitute other bubbly drinks, like sparkling cider, for our celebrations. That's why we've got two champagne fountains here tonight—alcoholic and virgin!"

Everyone laughed at the reference to virgin. It gave me a flashback to childhood and my first kiddy cocktail I had in a Miami restaurant when traveling with my parents. I think they called it a Shirley Temple. I was more interested in the tiny umbrella and the ultra-sugary cherry than the contents. I was even a virgin at the time. I was smiling at the thought of what a small percentage of my life that was true.

When talking about *Responsible Sex*, Dana made sure she stated from the beginning that immortalists are not prudes—far from it! She talked a little bit about sexually transmitted diseases, and how she felt these were but one challenge manifested on Earth to help us consider a new relationship to our sexuality. The disease AIDS brought to our consciousness and research labs much work on the subjects of both our sexuality and longevity. Thanks to the commitment of those dedicated to this work in the medical and spiritual communities, AIDS often could be prevented or arrested.

I was so sorry that wasn't true for my brother Gregg, but I had to celebrate that he lived a decade past his diagnosis. If I had been sitting next to April, I'd have squeezed her hand in honor of her father.

Dr. Dana next cited the sexual revolution of the 1960s and '70s as an important evolutionary phase to help people overcome years of cultural repression concerning sex. That accomplished, however, then came the more elusive frontier, the achievement of true intimacy. She talked about how sexuality and intimacy are often confused—how sex can sometimes masquerade as intimacy. Sometimes frequent, great sex helps couples avoid deep communication with each other. Because of the physical closeness, there is an illusion of emotional closeness, which may or may not actually be there.

I considered how much of this might be true for Curt and me. I'd have to come back to that one and meditate on it.

"The question to ask yourself in any sexual encounter: Is this consensual? Am I using this person in any way? What is the communication?"

Dana emphasized that sex is a powerful vehicle for expressing love and the life force. Because of the vulnerability involved, we must always, for our own sake and the sake of our partners, share sex with the most loving consciousness.

"Sex is also one of the world's greatest forms of recreation," Dana stated." Curt elbowed me then gave me a squeeze.

"In IOPEA, we make even more conscious choices about *procreation*. For immortalists, the birth of children is a serious decision, because our children are likely to live a long time, raised in our way of life. We teach conscious contraception to avoid contributing to world overpopulation — and conscious *conception* if you choose to become a parent. Because of our belief in the importance of parenting on purpose, IOPEA has been active, along with many other nonprofit groups, in making planned parenthood education readily available worldwide."

On the topics of *vegetarian* and *fasting*, Dana talked about the physiology of human beings and how many committed vegetarians argue that we were never meant to be meat-eaters — a habit that got started along the way, by a supply problem, that simply stuck.

"There remains controversy about whether or not the human digestive system was designed to process animal meat. There is the issue of eating food that is (excuse the expression) dead and which got onto the plate by an act of murder. Spiritually and physically, meat may not be the best food for us."

Dana discussed her own conversion to vegetarianism, and how, to her surprise, she found life still delicious, once she learned new ways of shopping and cooking. "The occasional fast is a way to rest the system and to cleanse it—also to do spiritual work, since it focuses us away from the body. It makes the head lighter and more open to divine inspiration. These simple health techniques keep the body tuned and flexible. Besides, how often do you see a fat vegetarian?"

When the centaur pointed to *Bathing*, the board lit up a scene of a group of people soaking in a hot tub. "If you ever want to find a group of immortalists, start looking for the hot tub," Dana advised. "I'm surprised we don't all have dish pan body."

She explained that showering and bathing cleanse not only the physical body, but also the aura—the invisible human energy field—from any negative vibrations picked up during the day. "Besides, hot water is extremely relaxing and with a bit of proper breathing, can lead to spontaneous emotional release experiences." She threw in a little advice about how to mix bathing with aromatherapy for heavenly results. I could almost smell the scent of lavender ...

Gravity found the centaur hanging from the white board by his hooves, upside down, pointing to the word, topsy-turvy.

"When we talk about gravity in IOPEA, we mean two things that can make your entire being sag—gravitational pull and too much seriousness."

"For this reason, you'll often find us hanging upside-down from back swings, monkey bars in our back yards, or standing on our heads in yoga sessions. This not only helps circulation; it reverses some of the downward pull that can leave you jowly—or for women—sagging in places you used to be perky. When we're not defying gravity in this way, you'll find us doing it the other way—laughing."

Forgive opened with the cartoon centaur snatching the flower Dana was holding in her hand, and then saying he was sorry. Dana said, "I forgive you."

"Forgiveness is more than accepting an apology. It doesn't mean being a doormat, that you shouldn't protest behavior you don't like or think is oppressive. What it does mean is 'then was then, and now is now.'

You don't need to tolerate being dumped on. You don't have to be friends with people who treat you badly. For your sake and theirs, however, it's golden to let bygones be bygones and to respect the humanity of the person behind the foibles. When a person is being the most obnoxious, his or her cry for love is the loudest. Try returning love, and watch the whole scenario change before your very eyes.

Grudges will literally kill you, and learning forgiveness is indeed a critical lesson in long life."

By now, the centaur was becoming a ham. When *Fear* lit up, his teeth began chattering and his legs wobbling. Onto the screen was projected a highly suspenseful scene from a horror film.

"Life may have at times *felt* like a horror movie to you. This may sound even more shocking than some of those thrillers you have watched, but it is *literally* all in your mind."

I figured I'd better listen up on this one, as I'd given myself a film festival of horror flicks in my head since this morning.

"The instances where a person is being actually, bodily threatened in some way, compared to the number of times we pump adrenaline, scaring ourselves silly with our own thoughts, are minuscule."

From her mouth to God's ear, I thought. I hoped I'd be able to figure out the difference tonight.

"In IOPEA, we teach you to respect and listen to your own intuition. Your inner voice will scream loudly and clearly when it's time to duck, or if there's a plane that's about to crash. Follow your 'bad feeling' and change your reservation.

The rest of the time, we teach you to skate. You are beloved of God/Goddess/All That Is—however you perceive the Ultimate Life Force. In learning to trust that force fully, we actually attract more love and protection to us and dispel negativity."

Active opened with a group of older folks jogging down a beautiful lake path. Dana said, "Even if you've aged to senior status before embracing immortality, it's never too late to rejuvenate!"

Dana talked about retirement as a thing people do when they're waiting to die, the same people who are looking for an "end" to their struggle instead of learning how not to struggle in life. She advocated working indefinitely. "When they finally kick you out of a 'real' job, take your pension and other benefits and run—to do what you've always wanted to do, whatever that is."

"While there's still only a few of us immortalists, we won't bankrupt the system," she mused, imagining the cumulative effects of nonstop Social Security. "Later, we may have to up the age for collecting full Social Security benefits to 100 or so."

Laughter.

Lastly, the word *Imagine* lit up on the centaur's board, to the tune of the old John Lennon song about peace.

"The power of your imagination is the Fountain of Youth. To live long, you must see yourself as an eternal being. To have a world worth living in, see it in peace and harmony. As to war and disease, we at IOPEA constantly imagine a world where both are eradicated, a place where people live together well and die when they're done."

I was up again on the voiceover.

"These paths to immortality are just a taste of the ways we create long life at IOPEA. We look forward to teaching you more techniques to make you last long, if you decide long life is for you."

The next segment was the much-awaited and most exciting part of the video: IOPEA's score card for social change.

Even after Dana's cheerleading, I heard only bits of what followed. The "secret of immortality" section was over. As promised, I had given no new info to Foy. I tried to listen, but I was lucky to hear half of the rest of the movie. I could tell Curt was getting antsy with the long program, and I knew we still had the New Year's ceremony and costume contest yet to go. I managed to pick up key snippets of IOPEA's accomplishments:

"IOPEA's overall strategy concentrates on six areas for reform: education, family services, economic distribution, health options, ecology, and mass communications."

I was back narrating the film, explaining the two key tools that enabled IOPEA to do so much in such a short time: ongoing generous membership contributions and our cable network, Colorful Life Media.

Back in my seat, I daydreamed till I started talking on video about my favorite program. It's hard to watch yourself in a movie. I was starting to get bored with myself. I hoped it wasn't contagious.

"Recognizing the power of the media to convey many of the societal changes they longed for, IOPEAns voted overwhelmingly to purchase a cable television network as our first major investment."

This introduction led to an outdoor shot of the Colorful Life Media station, then inside to the set where *I Am Special!*, CLM's daily self-esteem show for children is taped. The nearly all-kid cast ranged in age from preschoolers through teen-agers. The *I Am Special!* regulars had become as familiar to CLM's younger viewers as the original Mouseketeers had been to their grandparents in the 1950s.

I Am Special! focuses on teaching children of all ages to value themselves and each other and on conveying the importance of cooperation and shared power. This perspective is balanced with a strong emphasis on individual creativity. It features parental involvement segments, an idea suggested from one of our member's days in the peanut gallery of early-TV kid shows—specifically, from *Ding Dong School* with Miss Frances and the program segment, "It's time to go get your mothers."

The writing co-op felt that an inter-age and intergenerational format was important. By keeping brothers and sisters aware of the concerns and feelings of their younger and older siblings, they'd understand each other and get along better. This seemed important, as the spacing of children had gotten wider and two working parents, the norm. The regular appearance of parents and teachers on the show also keeps the lines of communications flowing between youngsters and their grownups.

I Am Special! had become a positive addiction across America and English-speaking countries where it has been exported with great success. New translations are being added annually. *I Am Special!* is now delighting viewers worldwide.

The show's head writer, Max Kidd, appeared to say:

"*I Am Special!* has one goal: to eradicate poverty, child abuse, drugs, and ignorance by teaching children their intrinsic value. It stops the cycle of passing on these problems. Like the Little Engine Who Could, children taught to love and believe in themselves simply cannot fail in the larger sense in life.

I Am Special! builds confidence in kids—a sense of ethics and self-value. We teach children how to think for themselves, so they come to understand from an early age that the solution to all their challenges lies within them. We teach them to listen to, and honor, that small voice inside them that is truth."

So, here's your truth, Foy. I hope you can hear it—and honor it.

I hoped against hope that if we could teach this to kids, we could teach it to one apparently misguided and hurting grown-up.

Chapter 22

Hans Jenner had offered to handle the tree ceremony, the beginning of the events leading up to midnight, bringing in the New Year and the next quarter century of IOPEA. Hans and I had barely spoken since our calls earlier, but we managed a quick exchange when he first arrived at the Ball.

Hans was decked out in his impression of our futuristic, intergalactic currency, a one-dough-fits-all legal tender he called the galactico. He was wearing a tunic with a blow-up of the 100-galactico space note. He had other denominations glued to his long t-shirt sleeves that peeped out underneath. His whole get-up was primarily green, including a space helmet with his self-created symbol for the galactico raised, three-dimensional, and painted gold above his face shield.

"It's supposed to be two hands touching at the base of the palms, opening to receive money or prosperity," he told me. It looked to me more like the glyph we used as kids to depict a bird in our rudimentary line drawings—or, as an astrologer, the symbol for Aries with both wings pulled down to make the "V" more open.

"The perfect choice would have been star bucks," Hans said, "But obviously, the United Galaxy would have a trademark issue with the coffee company … although I bet they'll be the first coffee chain on the Moon."

Back to Earth, the Immortal Millennium Tree was a black cottonwood, also known as the California poplar, a species with lore for long life. Several helpers moved it to the front of the ballroom in a giant wooden tub on wheels. Besides its folklore association with longevity, I love the cottonwood's heart-shaped leaves.

The Four Elements were back in on the act, passing out little silver tubes that resembled medicine bottles with caps and green loops for hanging them on the Immortal Millennium Tree. Each tube contained two strips of paper for writing one's wish or wishes for the future. Pens and extra strips of paper were passed around in another basket for those who needed them.

The tree was meant to be a living time capsule. Hans told everyone that they were welcome to pull down a new millennium wish from the cottonwood tree, once it was planted near the entrance at IOPEA headquarters, any time they needed inspiration or a positive affirmation for the future.

"Let's have some of you come up here and share your wishes for the future with us," Hans invited, holding out the microphone to encourage takers.

The first partygoer's sentiment was one everyone shared. It received a booming round of applause: "The end of all war."

Dana's wish seemed to match her soft sculpture rainbow, glued to a red body suit, making her a thematic match to the opening of the movie we just watched: "That each of our most heartfelt dreams comes true." Out of her white lab coat, Dana was now just another IOPEAn, wanting to live long enough to see her personal visions realized.

I added, "The freedom of all spirits and their creative expression."

Reggie wished for eternal beauty to all creatures on Earth, and the continued joy he received in helping make people beautiful.

Laurie-Ann Van Kekerly, a member who belonged to an all-woman group of stilt walkers from Berkeley, explained the meaning of her silvery costume in her wish. "I wish that all people would *feel* as tall as I *am*." Laurie-Ann played one of the grown-ups in the neighborhood in the IO-PEA children's program, *I Am Special!* She was walking her talk tonight.

The steady stream of well-wishers continued for more than 15 minutes. Toward the end of the procession, the Brain wished "that people would use as much of their heads as possible, including both the creative and analytical halves of their brains." His girlfriend pitter-patted behind him, adding, "I want all people to learn to trust their hearts."

Who were these kids? They talked as if they were reading right out of the *Immortalist's Handbook*. I'd have to ask someone who they belonged to. My guess would be some dyed-in-the-wool IOPEAns.

Curt didn't have the nerve to go to the microphone. I wondered what his private wishes were. I swallowed hard and with difficulty, remembering that in hours, we'd have The Talk about our future together.

Even Don Winter announced his wish: "I wish I'd have as much fun as I've had tonight for the rest of my life."

I'd like to help you with that, I thought to myself.

After everybody spoke who cared to share, Hans announced it was time for the remaining well-wishers to line up and place their tubes on the tree. Because there were hundreds of people at the party, the poor cottonwood's boughs began sagging severely, three-quarters of the way through the ceremony. On top of that, there was hardly an inch of branch left for carrying the last batch of silver tubes.

Hans had a fabulous idea. "Is that Tree Man still here? Want to come up and carry the overflow? Our cottonwood just ran out of room for all these good wishes."

The Tree Man scurried to the side of the Immortal Millennium Tree as fast as his feet could carry him, in baby steps, inside his narrow, soft-sculpture trunk apparatus. He reminded me of my early days, learning to walk in high heels and a tight skirt without enough slit and freedom of movement.

Tree Man looked thrilled to become the second Immortal Millennium Tree of the evening. As the Four Elements wheeled out Tree #1, the audience applauded the main bearer of their affirmations for the future, while Tree #2 bowed as best he could and received another round of appreciative clapping. The medley of tree ceremony songs ended with "I Wish You Love."

Before the final bars had faded, Reggie appeared at the microphone, in a change of costume from his earlier photographer's get-up—a hat with a PRESS card stuck in the band, several cameras around his neck, and an umbrella photo light on wheels that he walked like a dog throughout the party. Now, Reggie was dressed in clown make-up and hair with a literally painted-on, ear-to-ear grin. His shirt appeared to be the top half of a clown suit, cut at the waist, and he was wearing a fedora and vintage suit, so that he looked half-clown, half-gangster.

He removed a gun from his holster, shot it with a big bang, and a red flag with white lettering popped out that said SMILE.

Reggie also carried a case. I imagined the gangster half of him had filled it with cash from his latest bank heist.

"I s'pose you're wondering who I am," Reggie said, hanging tough. "Well, dig it, I am the Grin Reaper."

Everyone laughed.

"You know those photos I was snapping earlier, when I was in photographer drag? Well, those weren't whole faces I was taking. They were *smiles.*"

"So, for the rest of tonight, as long as you can last at this endless party, we're going to pass out these little pictures with sticky tape on the back. They're the pictures of the smiles I've been taking."

The Elements appeared around the room with baskets, ready for their cue.

"You each slap on a smile on your shirt or costume, and your mission for the rest of the evening is to find whose grin you're wearing. When you find the source of your smile, find one of the Four Elements, and they'll have a little Happy New Year present for you from IOPEA. Good luck, Happy New Year, and Happy IOPEA's Silver Anniversary!"

The prizes were key chains with a ballroom globe.

The crowd loved it. The "grin and bear it" caused so much silly, Reggie could hardly get everyone to settle down for the next phase of the program—the Best Costume Award.

"Later, later, loves. You'll have plenty of time to find your grinner once we hand out the best costume prize. So settle down, and let's hear the verdict of our judges!"

Someone in a judge's robe entered from stage left while Reggie announced, "All rise for Hiz Honor!"

As the crowd scrambled to their feet, the judge handed Reggie a huge envelope, about two feet by three feet, with a big IOPEA seal on the back. The envelope was dressed up to look like an oversized facsimile of the ones used at the Oscars.

"The envelope, please," Reggie said.

When he pulled out the contents, a fanfold of paper fell to the floor. The announcement looked a mile long. Reggie began reading.

"This was a tough job. There were three judges, and we almost went out of our minds, trying to *make up* our minds. We couldn't come up with just one winner, so we finally compromised on a tie for first place and a bunch of honorable mentions."

"So, here goes," Reggie said. "First honorable mention goes to our beloved Micki Michaels, President of IOPEA, who reminds us tonight that our beliefs change us down to the most microscopic cells of our bodies. Evolution occurs in our DNA, including the slowdown of the aging process and making claim to a full, rich, and long life. Also sharing this honor and round of applause is Ira Miller, Micki's costume creator. Micki and Ira."

I wanted to low-key it in favor of others, so I stood up at my seat in the front row rather than rushing up to Reggie. There was long applause and obvious appreciation. I turned around to see my favorite gadget guy, looking uncomfortable in the limelight. I couldn't help but notice that Loni was beaming beside him in the back row over this double shot of pride by association.

"Second honorable mention goes to the ensemble, the Intergalactic Security Checkpoint—your *flight to the future* security team. You remind us that there's no place in our future for weapons—plus you were so convincing, most of us thought you were real cops. Please, come forward!"

I could hardly contain my laughter watching Curt's ragtag squad rush up, slap each other on the back, and give each other high fives. Curt, Tansy, April and Brady were nearly falling off their chairs howling. The fact that we'd pulled off the "fake" security act so convincingly left me bursting with relief and hilarity. I couldn't look at Curt, because I knew I'd fall into one of my uncontrollable fits of laughter, the kind that won't stop once the room is quiet. I really didn't want all of IOPEA to think they were being led by a laughing hyena or to risk another one of those stress incontinence moments. There were two things that gave me a weak bladder—fear and uncontrollable belly spasms.

"Third honorable mention goes to the Four Elements—Earth, Air, Fire, and Water. You remind us of the stuff from which all life is made, the seasons of change, and the way all these forces must work in harmony for a well-rounded life. Best of all, in your helpful role all evening, you set a beautiful example of the commitment of all IOPEAns to planetary service."

The quartet assembled in the spotlight, bowing together like professional performers, stretching it out and hamming it up almost as much as the cartoon centaur in the *Immortal Millennium* movie.

"Our fourth runner-up is Dana Porter, for the beauty and creative execution of her costume, and for her reminder to us to look to the rainbow. The rainbow has been the symbol of happy endings throughout history. The rainbow is the gift after the storm. The rainbow is a symbol of our beloved centaur Chiron. It symbolizes the bridge between inspiration and form. The rainbow reminds us of our mission to bring inspired creativity into the 'system' of society, finding evolutionary ways to make it work in harmony and equality for all."

"Two final special honorable mentions go to Mack Coswell, better known as The Tree Man, for his impromptu help in saving the sagging boughs of our Immortal Millennium Tree by offering to carry the overflow. We'll put all the extras in a weatherproof chest in front of the cottonwood at headquarters. As our silver anniversary tree grows, we'll hang the capsules Mack carried tonight on the Immortal Millennium Tree Annex. Mack."

Mack once again baby-stepped to the spotlight from the nearby sidelines, where he had only recently waddled after being weighed down with the remaining silver tubes.

Reggie hesitated to read the final honorable mention. To the judges, sitting nearby, he said, "Come on, you guys. I can't read this."

Someone suggested he hand it to me.

I ran up and read, "To Reggie Roland, who is instrumental in concocting faces anybody's mother could love and complementing costumes with sheer genius, giving them their final touch. We honor your special place in IOPEA and our hearts. Especially, we thank you tonight for taking a deathly concept and turning it into something brimming with life in the Grin Reaper. Long life!"

I'm sure Reggie blushed under his already fire-engine-red cheeks. I asked him if he wanted to continue to read the winners. He did.

"Now, for the moment we've all been waiting for—the winners!"

"In choosing our winners, we emphasized not only the creativity and execution of the costume, but its message as it applies to IOPEAn philosophy. With those elements combined, our hands-down choice was the Brain and the Heart, for reminding us all that only when these parts of ourselves work in harmony, are we fully alive. Come on up here you two. You also win for the most anatomically correct costumes!"

The biology class couple tripped up to the front hand in hand. Everyone yelled, "Speech, speech!"

They both shook their heads, and after much coaxing, the Brain said, "We just want to say *thank you*, and we're glad you thought our costumes expressed well what IOPEAns believe."

Despite their shyness in accepting, the applause meter nearly broke in aftermath of the Brain's brief statement. Who were these kids?

Reggie added, "Your prize is a $1500 travel voucher to use to book travel anywhere in the world, donated and sponsored by various IOPEA members in the travel industry and supplemented by the headquarters special events fund." The assembly clapped, and many of them oohed and aahed enviously. I thought about the fact that if we were right, future prizes of this sort would be purchased with gallacticos and not limited to Planet Earth.

"All of our honorably mentioned will receive a pair of tickets each for free dinners at the famous San Francisco vegetarian restaurant,

Crops, owned by IOPEA's own Sam and Sandi Green."

"Now back to slip you her usual mickey of love and laughter, one that will knock you out in the best possible way, is our illustrious leader, Micki Michaels."

I took the microphone from Reggie and outlined what was happening next.

"The best costume awards were the last scheduled program before we welcome in the New Year, just a few minutes from now.

After that, we're by no means done with you. We hope you'll dance till dawn!

For the rest of the evening, we've arranged for our own facsimile of The Wolfman to play you what we call The Top 40 from the Last 50-Plus—top 40 hits from the last half of the 20th century. Only watch it, ladies. He's a wolf in the bad boy way."

Hoots and hollers from the members of the audience that, like me, were older than they looked.

"But before we pull out the noisemakers—they're in bags taped to the bottom of your chairs—let's have one last meditative moment before we welcome in the New Year and next twenty-five years of the Immortalists on Planet Earth Association. Please sit up straight, get into your meditation posture, and take three deep breaths.

Envision our beautiful planet with a gentle shower of stars of peace bringing blessings and wisdom from the heavens. See the people on Earth joining hands, sending the love in their hearts around the galaxy and through every speck of space. See this intention cleansing our earth to its very core, and filling it with love—always."

I had to cut it short. The program had run long, and it was at 11:59 and almost no seconds. I could hear Cosma in my mind, letting me know in her sweet, matter-of-fact way. She had branded me with a time sense I'd never known before her. Cosma honed my time intuition.

Gong Guy had been instructed to chime in the New Year, using his cell phone as his guide, since mobile phones are satellite synched to precise time. Thankfully, the Gongster had left behind his earlier, eardrum busting percussion tool and was using a huge Tibetan-singing bowl to strike the exact moments that would usher in the New Year. At twelve seconds before midnight, he'd make his first bold tap to the side of the reverberating bowl. The twelve taps and singing sounds represented both the twelfth hour and the countdown of the last twelve seconds to midnight.

With their eyes still closed, I saw the meditating audience stir as something fell on them gently. As they opened their eyes, thousands of tiny, silver paper stars were falling like a winter snowstorm on the gathering. Gasps were heard throughout the room as the lights were brought up just enough to catch them glimmering down on them.

The musicians played "The Peace Song." As the throng sang, the faux ceiling once more parted, yielding a downpour of balloons, streamers, and confetti—all of recycled materials, of course. To add a visual exclamation mark, I flipped the switch and lit up my flashing DNA spiral.

The band shifted gears for a medley of merrymaking music, beginning with "Auld Lange Syne" and ending with "To Life!" By then, they were revved up for full-tilt merry. The real party had just begun.

Chapter 23

It was almost 12:30 AM, according to Cosma in My Mind. Had I dodged a bullet, either literal or figurative? Was Foy all talk and no action?

We'd gotten through my speech with only a threat. He had made no moves since the movie and welcoming in the New Year. Could I breathe a sigh of relief, or did no news mean bad news?

Curt sidled up to me.

"You're a DNA molecule and I want to smear you on a slide and find out who's your daddy."

I was sure I'd need a white cane before the night was over for the sprain I got rolling my eyes over that one.

"I need to sit," I said. We moved to the nearest cocktail table.

"Want a drink?"

"Sure," I said. "Make it the real thing."

As Curt took off for the champagne fountain, I collapsed into my seat and rubbed the back of my neck. I watched everyone dancing. I swayed internally to the rhythm. I started hoping for a second wind so Curt and I could join the fun. I loved dancing with Curt, especially slow dancing. It was vertical sex—the foreplay part.

I closed my eyes to shut out the swirl of visual stimuli and reground myself. Now that I'd stopped spinning, I was almost nauseous from all the sights, sounds and movements—that feeling like you're still moving when the merry-go-round stops. It reminded me of the first time I ever went into a boutique in the 1970's. I was on sensory overload, looking at all the items from floor to ceiling, including mobiles and psychedelic colors twirling.

Hello, backs of my eyelids. How are you holding up under the strain?

Just then, a psychic impression jumped onto my lids as clear as if they were small movie screens. I saw the picture in the beauty trade magazine of Oliver York visiting the cemetery and the graves of his father and sister. I had never had a photographic flashback quite like this before. I knew it was telling me something.

I simply scanned the picture. That's when I saw the detail on York Senior's gravestone that I hadn't noticed before. It said Francis O. York, Sr.

OMG! That's FOY—Francis Oliver York. Oliver York went by his middle name! He was Francis Oliver York, Jr.. All this time I thought Foy was FOY as in Fountain of Youth.

I let the images continue to unfold as the intuitive flashback reprised what I'd read in the article. The niece and nephew to raise. The swag placed specifically at our event. His Álainn cosmetics firm using Dickie Duh's warehouse. That had to be a sign that York's company wasn't doing so well; Dickie's operation was so under par.

Foy was trying to extort the "secret" of longevity to bolster his business. That had to be it! He was hurting, especially now with two kids to send to college.

But who was he?

Where was he?

And was he really dangerous?

When Curt came back with the bubbly, I was bubbling over with psychic impressions to share.

After I explained it all to him, he asked, "Are you sure?"

I was impressed that he actually seemed to be taking one of my psychic impressions seriously. The way my gut was throbbing, I said yes with confidence.

"What do we do?" I asked Curt.

"Stay very observant and watch for his next move."

While I restoked my hyper-vigilance, I watched the dancing, which was the main site of action at this stage of the Ball. I was charmed by Tansy and Brady, slow dancing in the sweetest way. They went well together. There was more tenderness than heat, which gave me a great sense that their world was right—and let's face it, a great sense of relief, too.

Next to them, the prize-winning Heart and Brain were getting as close together as their costumes would allow. They'd have stiff limbs before the night was out, since being swathed in soft sculpture cushioning meant holding each other at arm's length most of the time.

I caught a lock of the Heart's dark hair that had slipped out of the face opening of her costume. Then it hit me.

I finally saw the resemblance. All the pieces where meshing like gears in one of Ira's latest inventions.

"Curt, Curt! I waved my hands in front of him and tugged his sleeve.

"Curt, the Heart and Brain have to be Foy's niece and nephew. It all fits."

"You think?"

"I recognize her as the same catering girl who was staring holes in us when we first came through Security. And she fits the description of the young, dark haired woman who bugged Tansy's phone at O'Berger's."

Curt was on his radio in a flash, letting everyone know we had to zero in on the dancing biology team, the costume contest winners.

"Don't scare them off, Ace," Curt said. Next, he was telling Joe, "Be sure to go for Plan B."

"What's Plan B?" I asked.

"You'll see," Curt replied.

I saw Don and Ace circling the outside of the dance floor. Curt joined them, and soon they had the four directions covered, just like the Four Elements did earlier.

The Bio Team had switched partners with Tansy and Brady. The Brain was dancing with Tansy and Brady was dancing with the Heart. Everything looked normal, until I noticed that the Brain kept dancing Tansy closer and closer to the edge of the dance floor.

When it happened, it was faster than a flash, at a speed my own brain could hardly process.

Suddenly, the Brain pushed Tansy's arm off his shoulder, grabbed both her arms and twisted them behind her back. Out of nowhere, a man I had not noticed before who was dancing next to Tansy and the Brain, wearing black from head to toe, grabbed Tansy out of the Brain's grip and into his own. He started dragging her, one heavy arm under both of Tansy's, in the direction of the back exit, the door we were not using down the hall from the Green Room, AKA Reggie's place.

Then I saw it—a flash of silver. A knife in his other hand! He was holding a knife to her throat!

Worse, I saw a small red spot. The son of a bitch cut her!

My gun was out of my boot faster than a speeding bullet. Red exploded all over his forehead.

I shot the mother...

I ran to Tansy as Curt, Mary Beth, Don and Ace all converged on the fallen assailant. Don pulled out his handcuffs, I guess just in case I was my usual bad shot and the guy hadn't actually croaked.

Then my remorse set in.

"Book 'im, Don-o," Curt said.

"Book what? I just killed the guy!"

I couldn't imagine what people were thinking—my people dedicated to long life. I was horrified that I'd just taken another human life, even if justified. I was shaking. This had all just become my worst nightmare …

… and I realized, I had just witnessed the play-out of my nightmare of this morning—a man, shot between the eyes. People all around him in some sort of unusual costumes.

I had no idea I'd be the murderer. That I could murder. What was happening to me?

Curt came to the rescue. He threw out a verbal flotation device to keep me from sinking deeper into despair by setting me straight on what had just happened.

"Micki, you didn't pop him. You were too far away to do any damage. You probably shot the wall on the other side of him. He's not dead. He's just knocked out. Joe shot him with a paintball air rifle. That was Plan B."

"Paintball???"

"Yeah, that's his hobby. He's jacks up these rifles and goes to all the competitions. It's a way to keep up his sniper skills without hurting anyone. Something legal he can do with his sharpshooter abilities. Joe's one of the longest and best shots in the country. He likes to shoot guns, and these are relatively harmless.

"But the guy looked dead …"

"He'll have a helluva headache and a huge bruise, but he'll be fine. I think he passed out part from fear when he felt the paint hit and the splat. Probably thought it was his own blood and he was really hit."

"Joe could have used a color other than red. This looks real as hell."

I realized not only was I swearing more than usual; I had a room full of IOPEAns gaping at this scary-looking scene. I needed to compose myself, to step up to the plate—the microphone—and explain to them what was going on.

While Don finished cuffing the guy, Curt sent Mary Beth and Ace to the two exits—the one we were using and the back one we weren't—so no one could escape, especially Foy. Was he on the premises or did he call from offsite? The real cops, the ones on duty tonight, would want to question everyone present.

But my next move was toward Tansy.

"Are you OK, honey?" I asked as Brady held her close to him. April rushed to her daughter's side, leaving Ricky the Regressed Evolutionary Monkey, her latest dance partner, standing mouth open on the dance floor. Tansy, Brady, April and I huddled close, as Tansy told her experience.

"He barely hurt me, Aunt Micki. I was hardly scared. I knew Curt and his friends were all around." She held a tissue to the superficial wound and looked like such a brave angel bouncer.

"Yeah, including my dad," Brady said, eyes shining.

I wish I handled trauma as well as they did. I hoped it wouldn't be like whiplash where Tansy'd wig a few days down line. I'd be there for her and her mom, in case.

Just then, Don Winter stepped up after turning his cuffed perp over to Curt for the time being. He looked hot in his Intergalactic Security uniform— even in baggy, faded Dijon mustard yellow.

"Son, Tansy—are you both OK?" They nodded and reassured him. He hugged them.

"Micki—are you OK? Is there anything I can do?" He transmitted concern with his gorgeous green eyes.

Don touched my shoulder and repeated the question a second time. I was so overwhelmed with shock and body heat, I was dumbstruck. Especially when his hand moved gently up to my neck and rubbed it softly.

Curt marched back over to us, perp in tow, handing him back over to Don.

Apparently, speaking of me, Curt barked, "I'll take it from here." He put his arm around me and glared at Don.

Curt spirited me off to a corner.

"In case you haven't noticed, Don has the hots for you."

"How do you know it's not the other way around?" I grinned. Big.

"Do I have something to worry about?"

"I hardly think so. He hasn't owned major real estate in my heart since I was seventeen."

He gave me the face change.

"Just checking."

"Curt, this just scared the crap out of me!"

He hugged me. Long, hard, and slowly. It was better than sex.

"Micki, give me your gun. Now that the real cops are coming, they'll question us all and you aren't licensed to carry, much less concealed. Since it didn't do anything relevant, we shouldn't even mention the shot you took. If they find it on me with a round shot, I'll admit to the shot. It's my gun."

"What about my fingerprints?"

"We live together, Micki. It would be natural for you to handle the gun. You moved it when you were dusting stuff in our closet."

As if dusting in closets was ever going to happen at our house. Although, come to think of it, maybe Ira could program Hazel for that trick.

I handed over the Beretta, which Curt stuck in one of his multiple, inner raincoat pockets. I had never asked, but it was clear to me by now that his spy coat had to be custom-made. It had more pockets than a jeans factory.

As for the pistol, I was happy to be rid of it. The gun had served its purpose. It showed me in no uncertain terms that while long life was my intention, I'd be happy to shorten anyone's who screwed with my family.

"I have to go out there and say something to a room full of people in shock!"

I could hear sirens approaching. I'd better hurry up.

Chapter 24

I got word to Discarnate Voice, asking him to make a calming announcement while I gathered my wits and some words I'd need to pull out of thin air while thinking on my feet. At least the latter option would be easier with the iron out of my boots.

"Ladies and gentlemen," the Voice said, "Please take your seats and do not panic. The incident you have witnessed is not as bad as it looks. The gentleman was shot with a red paintball, not a real gun. Our illustrious leader, Micki Michaels, is on her way up to explain more. As there was an incident that provoked this reaction—more on that in a minute—the police are on the way. Please do not leave the ballroom, as they may need to question you. And by all means, don't let this ruin your evening. Please let it be part of the excitement."

Bob Blackstone was *good!* The man behind Discarnate Voice actually did have a history as a radio announcer and a current one as a bass in the IOPEA Life's the Gospel Choir. He had a sharp memory, too. He didn't miss a nuance I wanted conveyed with all the gentle authority his gifted vocal chords could muster.

Now it was time for me to rise to the occasion. There was a chance I might lose my job and the respect of my organization over this craziness, over the way I put everyone at risk, but I had to go out there and tell them the truth. I did not consult Curt. This was not about him. This was about being real, being honest and being me. For Micki Michaels, those three things are indistinguishable.

"Friends, San Franciscans—IOPEAns." I thought it best to deflect some of this drama with an opening bit of humor. "Lend me your ears."

A hush fell over the crowd.

"It's true; we've had a bit of an ugly incident here tonight. I was tempted to make up a story about it to spare you any concern. While pondering how to handle this just moments ago, I came up with a good one. *You can always tell them a local murder mystery dinner troupe is trying out for our next event!* That's not a bad idea. A whodunit dinner party would be fun. (Missy, make note of that for future consideration.)

I tossed that idea as fast as it shot through my mind. I have too much personal integrity and too much respect for each and every one of you, to lie to you like that, even in jest to protect you. Honesty has always been my policy as a person and as your leader. So here's the truth."

There was a buzz in the crowd. I'm sure speculations were being exchanged faster than phone numbers at a single's bar.

"Several key members of IOPEA—this goes most of all for me—have been receiving threats from a man with an Irish brogue who ultimately identified himself as Mr. Foy. This man's threats have been building until, today, he threatened to kidnap my great-niece, Tansy Michaels. He made good on that threat tonight by having someone grab her, brandishing a knife, who was beginning to drag her toward the back door of the ballroom. If it weren't for my boyfriend Curt Stern and his friends present tonight, who are ex-FBI agents and police officers, Foy would have succeeded in this plan."

I could hear more mumbling and see shock on their faces.

"Foy and/or his accomplices also threatened our IOPEA headquarters today—ransacked it. As you know, the office was closed for the holiday, and if it weren't for an intuitive tip that visited my psyche, we wouldn't have discovered the break-in until January 2nd. To make matters worse, the perpetrators roughed up our accountant, Virginia Goody, in the process."

The mumbling morphed to comments out loud, their faces from shock to wrinkled brows of concern.

"Virginia's all right, thank God. We'll communicate with you more on this incident early in the New Year. We're giving her time off to cope with her trauma, and she's being well cared for. For the time being, she's staying with Natasha Grayson and her daughter.

"How 'bout Sniffles?" someone yelled from the crowd.

"Snot ... I mean, Sniffles is with Curt and me until we can find him a cat-friendly foster home while Virginia takes a retreat away from the City. Catch me later if you want to volunteer."

Several hands waved wildly. Check that problem off my list. No more cat-choo! Curt would be grinning, if he heard that.

"What's this jerk want?" someone yelled.

"I was just about to get to that. Foy wants our 'secret' of immortality." I made air quote marks. "He apparently thinks there's some lotion, potion, pill or voodoo that helps us extend our lives and looks without any work on our part. If only!"

The worry gave way to laughter. Lots of laughter. I hope you're hearing this, Foy, if you're here. Yes, your belief in an easy-fix secret of immortality is laughable.

"Do you know yet who he is? Is he the guy that got shot with the paint-ball?"

"No, I don't think that's him, but I think that man is an accomplice Foy hired. I believe Foy thought his best bet was to kidnap Tansy. That I'd reveal the secret if her safety was threatened, because she's the closest thing I have to a daughter. Tansy would be held ransom for information he thought only I, or a select few others in IOPEA, could provide. And by the way, he also snatched the closest thing I have to a son, my cat Thusie. He was fortunately retrieved unharmed." More buzz in the crowd.

I had to think on my feet again. How much should I tell them?

"In answer to your first question, I believe—based on an intuitive impression and something I read in a cosmetic's industry journal today—that Foy is an executive in that industry, looking for an edge to increase his profits."

"Is Foy his real name?" the same guy asked again. Man, my poor father. This guy asked as many questions as I did when I was a kid—and I guess I still do.

"No. I believe I know who he is, but since there will be an ongoing police investigation, I don't believe I should reveal that hunch at this time."

"Is he in the room?" This was a new querant—Missy.

"Missy, we're not sure. If he's who I think he is, I've seen his picture, but people are in costumes here tonight. He could easily be hiding in plain sight. Now you know the reason for the Intergalactic Security checkpoint. We didn't want to take the chance that anyone could get in here armed. The tools were all real—the metal detector and wands."

"Then how'd that guy get a knife in?" Burly Blaster asked.

"Good question. That's one of the things we hope will come out in your conversations with the police. There was either a chink in our security or someone planted the knife in the ballroom ahead of time, before we set up the security point tonight."

Wow. How did I know that? Intuition sure startles me, especially when I have no time to doubt it.

Just then, the SFPD came busting through the door heading toward the stage.

"I see the Calvary has arrived, and I'd like to turn the mic over to the officers to instruct you further. Please, don't let this ruin your wonderful evening. Consider the interviews as taking one for the team and the longer night providing you with some extra entertainment you hadn't bargained for. It'll make a great story to tell your grandkids. None of us is harmed. That's the blessing we should focus on."

Four officers approached the podium. As they walked up, I imagined them as the Special Investigations Unit from *Nash Bridges*—Nash, Joe, Evan and Harvey. The reverie was so good; Detective Timothy O'Toole almost looked like Don Johnson when he introduced himself.

"One last thing before I turn this over to Detective O' Toole. I want anyone—anyone!—who had any contact from this Mr. Foy to see me before you leave the ballroom tonight. That means anyone you suspect might have been Foy or an agent of Foy. If you're not sure, see me any-way. I know you'll be telling these stories to the officers … but I have a need as your leader to piece together how this happened, as soon as pos-sible, for my own sake and for the sake of learning best how to handle any future, potential incidents involving our members and our work. I can't wait for the official police report. Please identify yourself to me as soon as possible, so we can all meet together before you leave tonight. I'll let you know where and when, depending on how the police interviews proceed.

Detective O'Toole …"

WHAT A LONG NIGHT. Detective O'Toole interviewed the knife-wield-ing suspect, as well as our in-house security team. He had his work cut out. Foy's thug had a long rap sheet. He was a goon for hire named Harry Hooligan. I kid you not. What kind of parent would keep a family name that bore such negative connotations? Harry should have sued his par-ents for child abuse. He was destined to turn out badly with a last name that's tantamount to troublemaker. I was starting to wonder about the significance of so many Irish men in this debacle, even the presumably good cop, O'Toole, not to mention the role of O'Berger's.

O'Berger's roll is a bagel, my mind said. I can't turn it off.

O'Toole had a lot of questions about what Curt and his friends were doing and got turfy and righteous about their taking the law into their own hands.

"When have you ever seen a crime prevented lately, especially with today's limited resources?" Curt said. "I wasn't about to sit on my hands while my girlfriend, her family and friends were threatened. I did what I had to do."

I was glad to be standing beside Curt to hear him sound so "my hero." It was my *Officer and a Gentleman* moment.

However, I could hardly bask in it before I was worried, thinking he should tone it down, lest he antagonize O'Toole. I didn't need another "show of Irish" tonight.

"Point taken," O'Toole said. I could feel the detective dismount his high horse and start making allowances for a brother in the fraternity of law enforcers, past and present.

The other officers divided the crowd into Those Who Had Seen Something and Those Who Hadn't regarding Hooligan's attempt to abduct Tansy. They started with the Had Seens and asked the others to hang out while they determined whether they needed to bother to interview them.

My IOPEAns didn't let me down. I was proud of them. The Hadn't Seens were soon making a party on their side of the ballroom, now that the real party was over, due to circumstances beyond our control. They were playing charades, drinking champagne, eating more gala goodies and seemed to be recovering swiftly from this unexpected side trip. Fortunately, the Ball was already touted as likely to be an all-nighter or close to, so no net reduction in anyone's sleep or early New Year's plans.

I had spent the hour since the cops arrived milling between Curt and his friends, still hanging with Det. O'Toole, and the other partygoers. O'Toole called for back-up. They soon arrived to duck Hooligan into the back seat of a squad car, my guess to go to the PD for booking.

During the course of my mother-henning around the ballroom, several people identified themselves as having had contacts with Foy or someone who might have been Foy or related to him: Tasha, Missy, Mary Catherine, our receptionist, and to my big surprise, Ira and my mother. Suddenly, I started getting inklings on why they were as thick as thieves tonight.

At some point, I couldn't hold out much longer without having to visit the restroom. I stopped by Curt and the brotherhood to ask him to meet me at the bathroom behind Reggie's again. My movie title memory bank never let me down for a good clip of wordplay.

"You know, honey, Same Place Last Year."

It was hard to believe a year had passed, at least technically, since we last dealt with my bladder and wardrobe needs—and their co-dependent relationship.

Getting out of the get-up wasn't nearly as hard as getting back in. I ripped off my helix, did my thing and squirmed in and out of my leotards in about half the time before Curt would show.

I was so excited! A breather. I looked in the mirror. Big mistake. I was a wreck. Hugging and hair raking and thinking I had murdered someone didn't do a thing for my looks. I repaired what I could, and exited the powder room …

… right into Medium Message. He was standing two feet from the door. I could tell he was no longer a walking pun. He looked sinister.

Medium sprang toward me, pushed me back into the restroom, slammed and locked the door behind us.

He ripped off and tossed his oversized turban. He kept on his eye mask.

"So, ye thought there'd be no consequences, ya did, to withholding the information I want? Clever, how you had your whole horde lie and laugh about it."

Crap. Medium was Foy! I'd guessed it and dismissed it. When would I learn? I shouldn't talk myself out of my intuitions! I still fell into that trap.

He lunged for me. I kicked and screamed. I was completely outclassed for size and butt-kicking skills. After a scramble, Foy grabbed me hard, pinning an arm behind my back, the same move Hooligan made on Tansy. He aimed a hypodermic needle toward my neck.

"Scream one more time, and I'll squirt you full of a virus that will age you almost before your very eyes. You're not the only person who knows scientists."

"There isn't such a thing," I said. "The diseases that bring on premature aging are genetic anomalies. And you may as well drop that stupid Irish accent, Oliver York. I know you've lived in San Francisco long enough to have lost it. That brogue is just an artifact you bring out when it suits your purposes."

In retrospect, I think I should have taken the advice I wanted to give to Curt about not antagonizing someone who currently had the upper hand.

"This virus is a brand new breakthrough discovery and hush-hush. Studying it will give us the secret to reverse aging in the future … but I can't wait that long."

I heard the doorknob wiggle. Thank God, Curt had arrived—and he must have been there long enough to hear me scream. Foy might have followed me to the bathroom but he wouldn't have known I had a date with Curt for costume realignment.

Could Curt get to me before this guy shot me up with something that might actually, God forbid, turn the President of the Immoralists on Planet Earth Association into a drooling, doddering old hag?

I heard a flashback from this morning at IOPEA headquarters, a loud shot from the other side of the door. I knew Curt was blowing off the lock. Foy turned his head in response to the shot. He took his eyes off me and lightened his grip for a millisecond. It was just long enough for me to yank back out of his grip and kick him in the groin.

Curt ran to him, gun aimed at his head.

"If you touched her in any way, you're dead." Curt cocked his gun.

O'Toole, Don, Mary Beth and Ace came running when they heard the shot.

Curt had already wrested a pair of handcuffs out of his trench coat. If I'd have known before now that he owned handcuffs, I'd have …

Down, girl.

"Micki, maybe you'd like to do the honors."

"Gladly."

Curt handed me the bracelets. I cuffed Foy with an eager ease that came from righteousness, not experience, since I had never handled a pair of handcuffs in my life. Francis Oliver York, Jr., AKA Mr. Foy, was officially out of my messy hair, about to be safely turned over to the SFPD as the primary or accessory to a variety of charges including assault with a deadly weapon and attempted kidnapping. Whether or not a decrepitating virus and some sort of germ warfare was also part of the package—the jury was still out. I'd have to run that aging serum claim by Hans. It wasn't a high priority now that the alleged juice was no longer aimed at my jugular.

"You know, Missy," Foy said back in character and full Irish brogue as

Detective O'Toole stood ready to cart him off. "I can't believe you're so thick for such a clever punster such as yourself. You weren't so quick on the uptake this time. I didn't think it was a big leap from 'the medium is the message' to 'the medium's been sending the messages.'"

I did a complete Curt Stern Face Change Sequence.

Chapter 25

You can come down to the police station, if you want to be present during York's questioning," Detective O'Toole offered. He didn't look like Don Johnson anymore. He was cute, but not quite as eye-catching as the other fair-haired Dons that had been present tonight in fantasy and in person, Johnson and Winter.

O'Toole was offering a professional courtesy to Curt.

"Thanks, Detective." Curt jumped in. "It has been a hellacious day for us, and I think it would be better if we checked in with you later to get a recap, after we go home and get some sleep."

"Suit yourself," O'Toole said.

Once caught, Foy/York transformed himself rapidly into a model prisoner ready to cooperate, probably hoping to strike a deal on lower charges. I wondered who he really was—sinister Foy or reasonable York? No doubt, like all of us, he was a mix of light and dark.

York started cooperating by confirming that the Brain and Heart, indeed, were his niece and nephew, Felicity Jones, age 17, and Francis Oliver Jones, 16, known as Frankie.

"They look older," I said, before I realized that this might be insulting to a make-up mogul, bent on helping people look as youthful as possible. "My niece and I thought Felicity was at least in her twenties."

"Rough lives, especially since they lost their second parent."

That's when my anger started to morph and empathy came crashing in. York was really only trying to help his family, and I had to appreciate his plight at some level. After all, for all intents and purposes, I had "murdered" someone who threatened mine.

I asked O'Toole, "What will happen to Felicity and Frankie when Mr. York goes to jail?"

"The boy will be lucky if he doesn't end up in juvie or locked up in the California Youth Authority. He helped drag your niece to a knife-wielding kidnapper, from what I understand. Kidnapping is a felony. Hooligan had already moved her without consent and threatened to inflict imminent physical harm. He even drew blood. Depending on strictness of interpretation, he'd already met the textbook definition of kidnapping, even though he hadn't gotten her out of the building."

I drank this in and felt both anger and compassion rising—two feelings that were hard to hold at once.

"Part of me would like to see you throw the book at that kid, lock him up and throw away the key. I certainly hope you have that in mind for York and Hooligan. But I can't help but wonder, on the other hand, don't you think Frankie was just doing what his uncle forced him to do? Personally, I'd like to know how truly complicit he was." I stared at York when I asked this question aloud.

"Juvenile authorities and Social Services are on the way. They'll determine the facts and what's best for each of them."

"Please," York said. "No foster care."

"It'd only be months for one, less than two years for the other, till they age out," O'Toole said. "Longer and not as nice if Frankie faces the juvenile justice system."

"Foster care breaks spirits," York said. "I can assure you, Frankie only did what I made him do. None of this was their idea. Neither of them deserves to have their lives ruined because their parents died and I was a poor substitute."

"I'm sure you won't mind if we add contributing to the delinquency of a minor to your list of offenses, " O'Toole said. York ignored him and continued.

"They have other relatives in Ireland, any of which would be thrilled for an opportunity to move to the US and care for them. Even though my business is faltering, I can come up with enough resources to bring their relations here and let them live in my house — or send Frankie and Felicity to Ireland, if need be — especially with the help of that nice travel prize they won tonight. Thank you, IOPEA." He looked at me, and then said to O'Toole, "I hope you'll let me work it out with my attorney."

O'Toole considered this proposal for a moment. "We'll see. They certainly deserve representation."

Part of me was livid — another part felt so terrible for the kids. I believed York that Frankie wasn't acting on his own, that he probably wasn't a willingly participant. My face was longer than this night turned out to be.

I whispered to Curt, "Is there anything we can do?"

"Micki, don't go all bleeding heart on me. Remember, this guy or his goons could have really hurt Virginia, Tansy — or you. Focus less on what happened and more on what could have happened. Foy — York — and his niece and nephew for that matter, have to learn that extortion and violence are not the way you go about getting yourself out of a jam. York might have even planned to jack you up for cash as well as the secret. After all, he's in hot water financially."

I knew Curt was right, but I still had compassion at some level for York's niece and nephew. Yeah, and even York and his alter ego Foy. The kids' costumes alone proved that, at some level, York "got" what we're all about at IOPEA.

Stop it, I said to myself. I had to "come to." I had work to finish.

I WENT BACK INTO THE MAIN BALLROOM for my meeting with those who had encountered Foy — or thought they had: Tasha, Missy, Mary Catherine, Loni and Ira. I felt like Hercule Poirot in the final scene of *The*

Murder on the Orient Express or any one of his movies or TV episodes, where he assembles all the suspects in one room and tells them what he has deduced about who did it and how the murder was committed.

Our meeting was slightly different. First, I could never act as high fallutin' and know-it-all as Poirot. Nor could I walk like I had a stick up my butt. Second, the circumstances were better. We had managed to prevent murder and kidnapping, if not mayhem. We knew whodunit and whydunit, but we were awfully short on howdunit. Since my favorite punctuation is the question mark, I had to know. Third, I didn't work on my own. I led a team, so the answers were scattered among us.

"Let's organize this chronologically," I said. "Who got weird phone calls any time before yesterday, New Year's Eve?"

There was a chain reaction of "I did."

"OK, you all did. Were these crank calls—heavy breathings, silence then hang-ups—or did the caller identify himself to you as Foy?"

Three crank confirmations from Tasha, Mary Catherine, and Missy. Ira and Loni confessed that he identified himself.

Ira stood up. "Micki, I couldn't feel more awful about what happened. He convinced me he'd kill you if I didn't turn over my set of your keys. He found out I had them because I work on Cosma and Hazel at times when you're gone—and I service the alarm system at IOPEA. Anything he could steal seemed better than ..." Ira broke down. Loni massaged his back.

Once Ira regained his composure, I simply waited to hear his full confession of the long string of threats Foy had made, increasing in frequency and intensity over the past several days. I could hardly fault Ira for caving over what he thought was a direct threat to my life.

Ira said, in finale, "He also forced me to put the bug and spyware in your phone the last time I was at your house."

"The day before yesterday, when I was working in my office while you were tuning up Hazel?"

"Yes," Ira confirmed. "You left your phone on the kitchen counter." His hands were shaking. "He'd already made me turn over my keys, that's why I made a point of coming to the house when you were home. I didn't have a way in, and I couldn't tell you why."

I got up and hugged him.

"Mishka," Loni said, as I stood before her and Ira. "He did the same to me—forced me to make the call to change the catering order. He knew our voices sounded alike from talking to us both. He commented on it.

He also knew that he could get to me by threatening you, Tansy and April—my only daughter and granddaughters! He said he'd hurt any one or all of you. I couldn't have it. He swore me to silence, especially with you. When he found out I didn't have a set, he made me tell who had extra keys. I remember you mentioned Ira worked on things while you were at work sometimes. I knew he must have keys." Loni heaved a huge, dramatic sigh and confessed, "I'm the one who gave up Ira."

The rest was easy to figure. Loni couldn't resist confiding in Ira, her conscience killing her. I'm sure she begged forgiveness, and they supported each other through their mutual remorse for their actions that were the least of two evils.

"Did Foy—York—visit you in person?"

"Not him," Loni said. "I talked to him, but the man who got shot was the one who came to my door. He was scary."

Ira nodded agreement.

"And, Mom, did you call my house and talk to Tasha when she was there and discovered Thusie missing?"

"Yes, sweetheart. She told me everything. All this is why I was so concerned about you tonight."

I hugged her, longer and harder than I had in years.

Just then, Curt joined us to break up our magic mother-daughter moment. He had stayed behind to walk Detective O'Toole and his prisoner to the squad car. To be honest, he probably did that so he could sneak a smoke.

"You'll tell me later what I missed, right?" Curt said as he sat down.

I nodded, walked over, sat next to him, and held his hand.

"So, these are my unanswered questions. How did a knife and a hypodermic needle get past our security—and how did Foy—York—and Hooligan seem to have the lay of the land?" I gave them the short version about how Foy jumped me in his Medium get-up and threatened me with some sort of alleged wizening serum.

"I just got the answer to that. I was there when York told Detective O'Toole."

Curt pulled his chair up a bit to get closer to the others.

"The cosmetics' rep that visited Reggie early today when he was setting up and brought the sample bags was another stooge of York's. He was casing the joint. The bags were made up special. He might have been the second guy, along with Hooligan, that was doing surveillance on our house, Micki."

"That makes sense," I said. Drat, the Earthy line was probably a prototype that would never see the fluorescent light of a department store shelf. I better horde my little pots of autumn make-up. They couldn't make up for what happened tonight, but at least they'd be a tiny consolation prize. On the second thought, maybe I should have Hans check them to be sure there's no aging chemicals in them.

Curt continued. "The knife was from the catering cutlery. York's niece Felicity got a job with the catering company and volunteered to work this gig, so she could slip Hooligan a knife from the on-site kitchen. None of us thought about the knives in the kitchen as weapons. We just figured the kitchen would be off-limits to guests and catering would notice if anyone went back there who didn't belong there and shoo them out."

"And the needle?" I had to know the last point.

"Felicity brought it in with her. The catering staff arrived before Ace and the others set up the metal detector. She just slipped it to her uncle, the Medium, after she signed off her shift early, saying she wasn't feeling well. She had stashed her costume in a big Macy's bag, so it'd look like she came here directly from shopping. Stashed it the back of the pantry till she needed it and changed in the Ladies'. She was so covered up, none of the other staff recognized her, I guess."

It was surprising how simple it all sounded, once I knew the whole story. I'd already figured out that Foy planned to kick out and escape through the bathroom window, had he succeeded in extorting information from me, rather than getting a swift kick in his low-hanging personal copying machine. I had no remorse over that, especially if that aging juice was for real.

Darkness still danced through the Ballroom window. When I caught a glimpse of the clock on the wall, it was pushing 6:00. Daybreak wouldn't be for almost another hour and a half on this wintry New Year's morning in San Francisco.

I felt like my senior year in college in my finals week. I had three papers due in lieu of exams. I was drinking the dregs of coffee to stay up all night, every night—the kind that I kept heating over ten times and tasted like battery acid. When I wasn't beating on my typewriter, I was beating on myself, wondering why I took courses that all required lengthy final papers during the semester I was trying to say *hasta la vista* to my alma mater for good. It was like volunteering to pay triple the toll at the exit. The Crystal Ball had taken enough toll on me for one evening.

"I think we can all go home now," I said. At this late—or early—hour depending on how you looked at it, no one could accuse me of being a party pooper. The other guests already had left in small clusters, once the police no longer needed them for questioning and they'd lost interest in their charades or recaps of this crazy night.

A buzz started about going to Mel's Diner for breakfast. Missy was the most eager. Miss Lemon had enough of my Poirot games, which was saying a lot. Lemon was ready for her orange juice and coffee.

Curt and I looked at each other. We love Mel's, but it was clear from my side; we were in no condition. I was Burned Out looking into the eyes of Fried.

"You guys go," I said. "I am so exhausted. If Curt doesn't take me home, the headlines tomorrow will read, *Longevity Leader Dies Young from Too Much Excitement.*"

Curt did not argue.

As we crawled into the Spider to drive home to Pacific Depths, one last loose end sprang to mind.

"What about Dickie Duh?" I asked.

"I suppose we can find out tomorrow from the cops. Surely, they'll ask York about the fax from the warehouse—why he used it and if Rawlings was part of his team. York might have just snuck in to use it early yesterday morning. Hanging out there for an hour to use it would seem easy to pull off. Doesn't seem like Rawlings stayed in his office much. You want to hear one of my intuitions for a change?"

"Sure," I said. I wanted to encourage Curt to hone his sixth sense and live from inner guidance.

"I think Dickie is just a duh."

Chapter 26

I folded a copy of my resignation letter into the morning *Chronicle*. It was stuck between some pages near the front, the ones reporting the latest crimes and other upbeat news—local, national, and global. I checked and was pleasantly surprised that there was no mention, even on the back pages, of the break-in at IOPEA headquarters or the incidents at the Crystal Ball.

When I refastened the rubber band, I could already envision Curt having a conniption. A few minutes later in the middle of his breakfast, he found the bait.

"What the hell?" he said, startled, as the single sheet of paper, still hot from my laser printer, floated onto his toast and eggs over easy, unwelcome as a colony of ants on a picnic. He grabbed it and wadded it up, but his curiosity caused him to unwad it the second he got a glimmer of what it said.

"Michele, what are you doing *now?*"

"Drinking coffee. You?"

I was peeking over my big coffee mug—the biggest one in the whole house. It looked like something Oscar the Grouch lived in. It was in the shape of a trashcan, something I had picked up at a waste management conference when I worked for the Environmental Protection Agency. It had a lid and everything, even a fake dent.

"Don't be coy. You know I mean this damn letter."

"So, you're surprised …"

"Surprised? I'm shocked out of my mind. Yesterday you were willing to risk the life and limb of everyone you love so your precious organization could have some kind of milestone event, and today you're *quitting?*"

"I know it seems strange on the surface. I got a second wind and was very agitated when we got home."

"I noticed," Curt said.

"That's why I spent the last hour meditating while you were puttering and cooking yourself breakfast. Here's what I got …"

"Do I want to hear this?" Curt covered his ears. I put down my mug, walked over to him, and gently removed his hands from his ears. I kissed him on the lips, and then sat in the chair next to him. Very close.

"The chase, the mystery—the whole Foy thing. Once I let everything settle, I realized I have never had such an adrenaline rush in my whole life. Curt, I was good at it … good at figuring things out and taking care of everyone."

"Yeah, sure you were. You could have gotten Tansy kidnapped or decapitated, and you tried to shoot the bad guy from across the room with a short-range pistol, not to mention that you probably couldn't pop an elephant at two feet."

"Come on, Curt. I had every confidence in you to protect my family and everyone there. You and your friends came through. Trusting you guys was a good decision. The gun was your idea. I never said I was good at guns. Besides, I was just learning. And some of my solutions were ingenious."

"Name one."

"I figured out the puzzle. I got who Foy was in the nick of time so you and your team were poised on the Heart and Brain and able to stop Foy's goon from snatching Tansy."

Initiate face change sequence.

"I'll give you that. And this is leading where? What do you intend to do with the rest of your life?"

"I want to become a private eye."

I should have been more careful in my timing. He had just gulped a mouthful of juice, which he sprayed all over me with some funny sounds that I recognized as a gasp slightly camouflaged by a gurgle. I was orange in spots, which, it's well-established, is not my color. Curt was laughing uncontrollably.

"What's so funny about that?" I wiped citrus out of my bangs with a nearby napkin.

"Micki, you have to have 6,000 hours of investigative experience to get a PI license in California. Do the math. If you worked full-time as a police officer or insurance dick, it would take three years. What are you thinking? No police department is going to hire you because of your age."

"I beg your pardon. I don't look a day over 30."

"You're not intending to falsify documents."

"I have something better in mind."

"I know I'm going to regret it, if I ask, but if I don't, you'll tell me anyway."

My lower lip got pouty. OK, I admit to batting my eyelashes just a little. It couldn't hurt to be a little flirty and get my tears to the surface in case I needed them. I really don't like to manipulate with feminine wiles. It's hitting below the belt ... but this was an emergency.

I looked at my fingernails. I was stalling. I learned good timing from my dad. I knew I had to lay this on Curt just right or the thud of the lead balloon would be deafening. Worse, he'd send my great plans packing.

"Curt, you have all the qualifications to get a PI license right now. I could work under *you*. I like working under you."

People talk about jaws dropping, but I thought Curt's was going to smack his breakfast plate and crack the crap china. (I really need to replace that.) His eyes got so big, I thought his cheap plate had company for dinner—a blue couple.

"Michele Nicole Michaels ..." Curt had only called me by all three names like my mother once before. He was very pissed at the time, as she was on the rare occasions she triple name called.

"I am retired. Get that? R-e-t-i-r-e-d."

"I know how to spell it."

"Well, that may be, but I'm not sure you understand the meaning. I'll get you a dictionary."

"Curt, you wouldn't have to work very hard. You could hire a couple of the guys from Coppa Spy to work the business ... a couple who want to make extra money. Just like Nash and Joe did with Bridges & Dominguez. Your friends could be the ones to supervise me. You'd just be my boss in theory. They could teach me stuff, if you'd rather be out on your boat reading a book or whatever."

"Michele, *Nash Bridges* was fiction. TV. This would be fact. Real life. Besides, I couldn't imagine who I'd subject to that assignment."

I glared at him, mulling for a moment whether to take the insult seriously or to flood him with facts instead. The second path sounded better to me. Work from a position of power, not weakness.

"Unless you were lying to me, you told me that your friends are fascinated by the psychic and astrological perspectives I could bring to investigative work. I know from overhearing their conversations: they all intend to do side work now that they're retired. Joe is already doing some security and Ace and Mary Beth both have talked about getting their PI licenses. Don's still on active duty, but if SFPD hires psychics, there's a potential gig. Think of the possibilities with my combined talents. I'd be a PI-2, private eye and psychic investigator."

How could Curt keep doing those facial aerobics, day in and day out? Without his features locking up into some kind of permanent disfigurement?

Just for insurance, I thought I ought to turn up the heat. I let my eyes well up. I started sniffling. I turned away.

It took a few seconds, but I got to him. I remembered an episode of

The Bill Cosby Show where Cliff demonstrated how to do crocodile tears. His lesson must have really stuck.

"Micki, don't cry. Why do you want this all of a sudden?"

I blubbered about burnout and needing to help people in new ways, and the demands of the IOPEA presidency. After two years, maybe it was time for Tasha to take a turn as the heir apparent. I'd remain a member and participate at a much lower level of intensity.

"You can afford to live without your salary from IOPEA while you pursue this new path?" Curt asked, ever practical.

"You know the house is paid off, thanks to my inheritance and dad's advice about real estate before he died. I have my federal pension from my career at US-EPA. I really didn't live off my salary from the nonprofit. I've been banking most of it to help Tansy through college. And for a rainy day."

Curt and I hadn't talked nitty gritty about my finances before, since we weren't co-mingling our money, just splitting expenses. He knew the house was paid off, but I think the fact that I didn't have to rely on my IOPEA income was a surprise—or at least that was my interpretation of his ever-flexible face.

Finally, I got to what I considered, personally, the biggest selling point. I told Curt how neat I thought it would be for the two of us to work together. To have adventures.

"We'd be like Nick and Nora Charles. Monk and Natalie."

"Lucy and Ricky."

"Don't be a pessimist."

I continued to sniffle. I pulled away from him, created more distance between us, and spoke between sniffs.

"I just figured we'd finally have something in common. Something we could do together, learn and grow from … something where you'd be able to show off everything you know for a change, and …" I was blubbering.

"Shhh. Don't cry. It's not an all-together bad idea. It has some merit. I like the part about being on top for a change. It has a nice ring."

At least he could joke about it, finally.

"I know it's not the only way we could do something together, but it's a way."

He took my hands and pulled me up out of the chair. I knew he was dragging me to the bedroom.

"This being on top thing has such a nice ring; in fact, I'd like to try it out. It beats the circles you run around me most of the time."

I followed him feebly, but I couldn't let him have the last laugh or first nooky without at least feigning protest.

"What makes you think I'm that easy? That you can just drag me to bed like a caveman to shut me up? I'm trying to have a serious conversation here. I hope you're not just shining me on or discounting me."

My mouth was yapping and my body pulling back just a little as he led me upstairs to the bedroom and pulled the shades. Why were we up so early anyway? Oh, I forgot. We never went to bed. Cosma chimed. I'd also forgotten to turn off the alarm.

"Good morning, Micki. This is Cosma, your multi-dimensional music, sleep, and information center. This is your 7:30 AM wake-up call. You are listening to 'Auld Lang Syne' at your request. The time at the tone is 7:30 AM and 55 seconds, Pacific Standard Time. Today is January 1st. Happy New Year!"

Should old acquaintance be forgot filled the room, and I accidentally bonked the button for Hazel when I turned off the alarm on Cosma. Hazel wheeled herself in.

"Coffee? Tea?"

"Me?" Curt offered.

"I think we're talking about cups of kindness at the moment," I said.

Before I could tell R2Maid2 it was a false alarm for the second morning in a row, I got this terrible case of the giggles. My life was just ridiculous. Goofy gadgets, a spy in good operating condition, who was reluctant to work, dragons slain, new mountains and a new career to climb.

"What's so damn funny?" Curt enquired.

"Everything."

I knew where I was going. I was going to be a psychic private eye — or something to that effect. I didn't exactly know how I'd get there, but I also knew I didn't have to figure that out today.

I pushed Curt down on his pillow, looked him in the eye and said, "These have been 24 of the craziest hours of my life. I hope you had half the fun I did."

Curt responded, "I had so much fun; I can't wait till we wake up again later to 'have the talk' about our future. Nope, can't wait. I have to at least give you the headline."

I gulped.

"Don't worry, it's good news — or at least I hope you'll think so. I put my condo on the market a couple of days ago."

I actually gasped.

"I'm ready to renew my contract as your sidekick for as long as you still get a kick out of me."

"But, Curt, selling the condo is walking the high wire of us without a safety net."

"I'm willing to chance it," he said. "You can't go home again — and my home is here — more each day."

I was having a hard time breathing through this revelation. The poignant moment became uncomfortable after falling into the turquoise wells of Curt's eyes for a third time. I was afraid of drowning. I kissed him playfully, with humor always my trusty flotation device … but as usual, our kisses quickly set fire, paying homage to the element where we spent more of our time, oblivious to the water imagery in my mind.

"You made this decision about the condo in sound mind and body, of your own free will, right?"

"Micki, you know I never roll over. I don't do what I don't want to do."

"I'm glad, but just for a minute, show me how you can roll over in a way I know you'll want to."

I grabbed him by the shoulders and started us on a trajectory that landed him on top.

For now.